In the

Disappearing Water

for Ingrid

with love,

Caroline   2/09

In the

Disappearing Water

a novel

Caroline Sulzer

Plain View Press
P. O. 42255
Austin, TX 78704

plainviewpress.net
sb@plainviewpress.net
512-441-2452

Cover artwork by Ann Rado
Title page graphic by Helen Fay
Epigraph from *Elizabeth Costello*, copyright J.M. Coetzee, 2003. All rights reserved. Permission of Peter Lampack Agency, Inc.
Quotes from *Dead Meat* copyright Sue Coe, 1995. Courtesy of Galerie St. Etienne, New York.
Author photo by Andrea Sulzer.

Acknowledgments

Special thanks to Rose Vekony for proofreading, editing, and attending to this book at various stages in its evolution. Your skill and insight have been fundamental, as is your friendship.

Many thanks also to Nancy English, fellow writer and friend, for your steady willingness to read and encourage my work.

To my family, my deepest gratitude for all you teach me.

Contents

... there is no limit to the extent to which we can think ourselves into the being of another. There are no bounds to the sympathetic imagination. —J. M. COETZEE

Longing

When she first met Hazel, Theo was working, erratically, on a doctoral dissertation that did not yet have a focus. She was unaware that she had recently conceived twins with M, one of her research subjects. Minutes after their children began, M told her the story of Aguja, the chicken he, for reasons he did not know, decided to save. He had named her Aguja, or Needle, he said, because she had briefly pierced his thick skin.

M worked in a chicken slaughterhouse in Northern California. Sometimes he was the cutter, the one who slit their throats. Other times he was responsible for putting the birds on the line or for taking them off and throwing them into the scalding pot.

He wanted, he said, to give one bird its life. But which one, when so many were moving by so quickly—and how, with all the other workers around? They might think he was stealing the bird for his supper or, worse, that he was soft in the head or, worst, softhearted. His impulse—you could call it desire—must have been too strong for these worries to matter. He even believed for a while that sparing one would help him kill the others. The reverse was true. Once he started looking for a bird and then when he found her, his job became almost impossible.

At the time it was his job to seize the chickens by the legs and hang them on the conveyor belt, readying them for the cutter. He became clumsy with trembling. He dropped birds as they struggled to get free. He said she'd squawked louder, struggled more fiercely than the rest. These were old laying hens, already sick and spent—and yet, how they still fought for their lives! When she hit the floor after escaping his grasp, she managed to flap her wings and stumble a few paces, though open space was scarce and her bones brittle.

She would be the one. M managed to grab her again, but gently this time and whispering, *I won't hurt you.*

"She understands me. I swear she understands me, Theo. I feel all her body relaxing."

He put her inside his shirt, and she scratched him only a little. After a minute she was completely still. I've killed her, he thought, then knew the quick heaving was her breath, not his own. He had only ten minutes left on his shift. We can do it, he told her. She nestled into his shirt, resting on the ridge of his belly, while he used both hands to send her sisters to their deaths. Her scratches, one right on the nipple, did hurt, he said, and helped him forget what he was doing.

When he got outside and was safe in his truck, he looked down into his shirt. *Hola,* Theo had imagined him saying to the bird, and then the bird stretching her neck a bit in response. At the sight of the small, almost featherless thing breathing into his chest, a horrible pity and revulsion must have risen in him. He threw the truck into reverse and then jerked it forward to the highway. The chicken squawked and flapped. She scratched his chest again, harder this time. He stopped as soon as he could and tossed her out the window and onto the shoulder of the road.

"I did it," M said, and shrugged his shoulders. He began reaching for his shirt, then his underwear. "*Completamente loco, no?* I don't know if I am more crazy when I loved her or when I hated her." He kissed Theo's thigh and stood to put on his jeans. The next day, he said, his grip was sure again.

    *

Hazel's story was longer than M's, and Theo learned it more slowly, over the course of the months they would spend together, while Theo and M's children took form inside her. Hazel and Theo had a few things in common—they both had parents who were immigrants, and they were both intimate with people who, at some point in their lives, slaughtered for a living. During this time, the time of Theo's pregnancy, aspects of Hazel's past became as vivid to Theo as her own reemerging memories.

Theo had never liked fairy tales, with their predictable structures and social hierarchies, but she did sometimes wonder: what does it take for the long sleep to be over? Even if she could not grasp happy endings, or transformation following on the heels of random cruelty, still, she possessed a strong, if innocent and intermittent, desire to wake up.

Childhood, she'd often thought, felt like a movie she did not remember well, or even like one she'd heard about but had never actually seen herself. To really see it she would, she knew, have to sit in the dark, alone.

1

After five years of not knowing his whereabouts, Hazel received a postcard of the Golden Gate Bridge from her father.

Walking back from the barn after putting the goat to bed for the night, she stopped at the mailbox and found it. The bridge emerging from (or was it disappearing into) a cauldron of fog. On the other side, his small awkward print.

I am thinking of you, and an address moving across the bottom of the card like the zigzag reading of a heartbeat.

Eventually, Hazel called information for a phone number but was told he was not listed. Then she decided to go to Maine, to the cabin where she and her parents used to spend three weeks each summer. She did not show her mother the card, saying only that she needed some time alone.

The water is wide, and I can't cross over, and neither have I wings to fly. Hazel sang the words of the song in her head as she sent breathy pennywhistle notes over rocks and across the water.

It had been five years since she last saw her father, five years ago to the month on this Maine beach where she would soon count cormorants and touch grief's old bone. She tucked her whistle into her pocket and looked out over the water. Someone was fishing from a rowboat darkened by the direct glare of the mid-afternoon sun. A lone figure stood in the small boat. The calm bay received the graceful line bending toward it, the hook invisible underneath.

She turned away, looking down at granite, schist, seaweed licked to brilliance by the tide, and began walking toward the distant mountains that sat, as ever, across the bay. The air thickened with her parents' voices and the heat of that

August, five years ago. Her bare feet sunk into clay, curled over barnacle-covered rocks, and found relief again in sand. It was as though she could see her own footprints from that time just now fading away. She could see her mother and father up ahead walking parallel, close then moving apart. The mountains, clearly visible at the start of their walk, had disappeared behind clouds by the time the two turned and walked back toward their daughter.

Hazel had reconstructed this day so many times in her own mind that she was no longer sure which details were exactly true and which had been added or adjusted at a later date. Perhaps he had told her mother then, as they walked under the gathering clouds. Petra, I will be leaving, he would have said in his low, musical voice, always the lover's voice—ardent and vulnerable.

Hazel was fifteen then, certainly old enough to be considered, to be told such a thing. But he had said nothing. Gabriel had not known himself what he would do. She had believed this for a long time. He was like a child, his wandering apparently as mysterious to himself as to those around him, a tic he could not foresee or control. He was a simple man, a hard man to blame. He had taught her to make music and to wrap her heart around each living thing. No one could say he hadn't done his job.

Now that she knew where he was, that he was alive, she had come alone to the place of their summers together to steady herself and to decide. The weight of his absence. The slightness of the card. They were irreconcilable. For a while she had waited for him, the way she had waited years earlier for her favorite cat to come home. When she stopped hearing her voice calling the cat's name into the woods, her voice turned inward, carving his name into a space inside, carving the end of hope.

The card was an assault. She would not be undone by it.

"Once you leave home," Gabriel had said to her, "you are condemned to wander. After leaving Ireland your grandparents tied themselves to the mast of a ship from hell with a few golden coins covering the holes in the bottom. And I still wander for them."

This was the closest he had gotten to an explanation for his periodic absences, which had begun before her birth. Why don't you go over? She asked him this more than once. Perhaps, he would say, looking past her.

Now she felt it—this absurd longing lying between them and joining them like that lovely, impoverished country neither had ever seen.

No one can know what shape love should take. Hazel believed this, too, for a long time. Wisdom, as a defense.

His driving away had not surprised her. Hazel knew that she could not predict how or when he would wander. But that he would not return, that she would finish her growing up and still he would not have walked through the door, this was something else. She and her mother did not talk about it. Whether out of wisdom or fear, their silence occluded the knowledge that her father had, in fact, done something common. Eventually, she would name it: a man had deserted his wife and child.

Hazel sat on the green schist boulder she'd sat on with her father five years earlier. She looked down into the small tide pool and watched a barnacle open and close. Sit and wait and you will see them open, he'd told her. She looked at the dry ones open now on the rock—rigid, silent O's. Watch them and feel your eyes, your blood, slow down.

The water was growing darker. Hazel had been sitting for some time. Gulls, a couple of loons, squaws, and other birds she could not identify sat, circled, hunting for food.

They held their conversations above and across the water, harmonizing with the sound of the waves collapsing in on themselves.

One cormorant stood on a rock, drying its wings. When it moves, I will go too, Hazel thought. She would enter the time of the cormorant, would sit and wait until she sensed without question it was the right moment to move on. Chilled, she hugged her shoulders and sat, resolute, watching the lovely black bird, its wings open and still.

The boat came so fast Hazel did not hear it before seeing it. It passed within a foot or so of the cormorant, close enough to almost tip the bird off balance before it managed to scramble into flight. Hazel stood up. The sun was just above the treetops on the other side of the bay. She watched it edge behind the trees gradually, then quickly in the end, leaving dabs and streaks of red in the clouds.

She walked on, along the bight that was a favorite for swimming, walking until it was too dark, under the new moon, to walk any further. She felt her way back over sand and rock, with the occasional camp light to guide her, and found, once she'd reached the cabin, that she did not want to go in. There it stood, a barely visible squat shape, as though challenging her with all the summers they did not spend together. She retrieved her sleeping bag from the car and lay it out above the high tide mark. In the morning she would return home, book a flight, and find him.

*

"That is not a toy," a woman said to her child, a girl of about two wearing a red jacket, unzipped and falling off one shoulder.

"You could get very, very hurt," she squatted to look the child in the eye, her back arcing next to Hazel's knees. "Darling."

Hazel stood watching the child, keeping an eye on the luggage circling on the conveyor belt. The girl was attempting to climb onto the machine, trying again each time her mother removed her. The child began to cry with a fierceness only children of that age can muster, and the woman, obviously out of patience, picked her up a little too roughly and carried her away, leaving their empty luggage cart behind.

Hazel grabbed her backpack and made her way toward the double glass doors and her first breath of California air. It had a subtle fragrance she could easily imagine her father settling into. When he left for shorter periods he had sometimes sent her postcards, as though he were away on a planned holiday. They had always been brief and upbeat, with no return address, ending with "I love you little faerie." She kept all his cards in a box, sensing that her mother would not want to see them.

A shuttle bus dropped her off at a city bus stop. Different colors of sky, same sky, different colors of houses—chalk blue, ochre, pale yellow, a peachy orange—warm, light colors of the south, though she was north. And so many flowers, blooming and apparently healthy in the midst of an incredible amount of traffic; these would have been enough to keep him. New York and Maine would seem sparse, stingy in comparison. Orange poppies sprouted on a patch of earth dividing the two sides of a wide avenue. A magnolia tree grew just by the shelter where people sat waiting for the buses. She picked up a fallen pink and white petal and felt its smoothness, then held it to her nose.

Traffic was slow over the Bay Bridge. She remembered pictures of this bridge rent in two by the last big earthquake. Her father had showed her and her mother the newspaper photo while they were eating breakfast the morning after the quake. Beauty has its price, he had said and smiled.

The bus wound its way through the narrow streets of the hills.

"This is your stop," the driver told her. "You'll need to walk a few more blocks that way." He pointed in the direction Hazel was to go.

She looked at the large house surrounded by a lovely garden gone a bit wild. He could never afford a place like this. As far as she knew, her father had never worked steadily for more than a few months at a time, and gardening did not bring in a lot of money. Of course, the gardening season here was much longer, and there were obviously a lot of well-to-do people who could use her father's services. Perhaps he was working furiously, sweating out whatever remorse he felt for leaving.

No one came to the door. She turned the doorknob, just to check. It was locked. There was no car parked in the driveway. Hazel sat down on the front stoop, suddenly very tired. Across the street was a lemon tree with many kinds of flowers growing to either side of it. The air smelled sweet, tinged with eucalyptus, the smell of that edge where longing meets hope. There were still several hours of daylight left; he was probably working and would return at sundown.

Hazel was not much for naming plants, preferring to have no words between her and them. Yet now she wanted to label all the flowers she could in what might not be her father's garden. She remembered walks with her father, kneeling next to a flower, him cupping his hand around it without picking it. They would look at it, at the different parts of it, noticing the scent, if there was one, in silence. He might talk to her about a particular plant, about its habits, which he'd come to know from spending many hours and seasons watching it. This is a dwarf iris, notice the three stamens projecting over the three falls; see how each leaf is curiously folded around the next younger. The iris needs space, and a little light coming to the roots. To learn names and facts he would have moved through the botany books and nursery labels with great difficulty. Letters and words refused to appear to Gabriel in their correct order, and so all writing was a puzzle.

Morning Glories. Poppies. Azaleas. These she recognized. Magnolia. Bird of Paradise. Columbine. She named what she could, and the names helped her to carve something precisely retrievable into memory. But she lost something, too, in the process. She felt this loss, as though she had captured something first poking its head out of the wilderness.

It was what she wanted now—to name them, to give distance, to look at a flower and not see the shadow of his hand cupped around it.

2

Theo stood among the children surrounding the animal enclosures. She held a cup of coffee, trying to wake up and to get warm. You are an addict, she told herself. Lift, she told the fog. The previous night had been long, sleep short and fitful. After M left at one or two in the morning she lay awake, looking out at the familiar patch of sky, glad he was gone. He had lingered longer than the first few times, which is to say at all, and told her the story of Aguja.

These children, this standing around and attempting to keep order, was a summer job, and served the purpose of augmenting her graduate student stipend. Children, their doomed beauty, frightened her, and yet she had signed on as a camp counselor, moving toward her fears like the shy kid raising a disconnected hand. Theo visited the animals in the park occasionally alone and today had brought the children on a field trip. The animals calmed her. She was not being judged. They were not waiting for her to say something or to answer questions like, How are you? or What's new? She watched a cow amble toward the children, heavy, unconcerned.

Theo knew her involvement with M was wrong, unethical according to the bylaws of the profession for which she was apparently in training. It was definitely not all right to get involved with one of your research subjects. What kind of science was that? Doubly not OK when you were training to be a psychologist. But Theo was not sure she wanted to be a psychologist. One day she might be a subject of her own research, which could involve further inquiry into dissociation. When is it a phenomenon of coping, even growth, and when a pathological symptom?

M had answered an ad for research participants that she'd placed in several papers. An interview was conducted in a professional manner, for which she paid him twenty-five dollars, and then they went out for a beer. Propped up on her elbows on the damp sheets, Theo had vowed not to see him again and to take her work more seriously. It wasn't the first time she had made such a resolution. In the early hours of morning, her body satisfied and coffee on the horizon, it was a supreme pleasure to reimagine her life.

A Holstein swept her tongue toward broken stalks of celery the children held out. Talk about ugly. A boy pointed to the cow's long, pale muscle. He dropped the food before she had a chance to grab it. Another, younger, child stuck out his tongue as far as it would go, comparing.

"It's ugly."

"It's white."

"Like a white snake."

Theo half stifled a yawn. A few children were feeding goats popcorn. Others were sitting on benches, eating. A chill fog hung in the air, and she couldn't get warm. She'd never be one of those cheery, fun counselors. Staying alert enough to keep her charges safe felt like the best she could do. She wondered for a moment whether this was the kind of weariness her mother had felt at home, alone with her children. But mostly M was on her mind, despite herself. Learn to juggle, she remembered his voice as he tossed each of their underwear and one sock into the air, and you'll be a happier person.

A tall young woman stood nearby, watching the children feed and tease the animals. She had long red-orange hair— the color of clown hair. She was a girl still, really, probably about the age Johanna had been when Theo last saw her. Johanna, her sister, who would always be eighteen, waving good-bye.

The girl, tall as Johanna, approached a boy who was offering a calf some of his hamburger. The calf sniffed it and turned away.

"Don't do that," the girl-woman said softly but firmly. "That hamburger is a dead cow. Did you know that?"

"Many dead cows," Theo corrected silently. That cow has ingested plenty of dead relations already. Everybody knew about mad cow disease, another disgusting fact that life went on around.

The girl with the clown hair knelt beside Evan, a pale, quiet six-year-old with dark red hair, very skinny. His parents were in the midst of an ugly divorce. Theo's boss had told her this, but it was there in Evan's eyes and posture, the way his head and shoulders curved downwards, as though he wanted to roll himself back up. He was her favorite kid. No one could offer a hamburger to a calf more gently and sincerely.

They could have been brother and sister, Evan and this young woman who touched his shoulder and said, "I know you didn't mean to hurt the cow." Evan stepped back and then lifted his wide eyes toward the stranger. This was why children frightened Theo. They could crack you open with a look. Evan ran to the nearest trash can and threw in the rest of his lunch. Then he ran back toward the girl who wasn't Johanna, eager to please.

"Are you the teacher?" the girl addressed Theo, smiling.

"No, I guess you are," Theo replied, with an edge to her voice. But when she looked at the girl, they both laughed, their laughter dispersing if not the actual fog, then something comparable within Theo.

"Here cow, here cow, here's your lunch," two boys shouted at Micah, an unpopular girl who often came to camp with bits of cereal dotting her full cheeks. The boys had been throwing lettuce at each other and then, bored with this, turned on the girl, waving the lettuce too close to her face. Theo watched, slow to intervene. Are you the teacher? She was aware of the girl-woman, their brief laughter still ringing, and also of something old that said, No, I am the girl. The voiceless girl.

Micah was on the verge of tears.

"What do you think you're doing?" Theo managed to say this to the boys, but without enough conviction to get them to stop.

The girl was crying now, her nose running.

"Stop," Theo wasn't sure she said out loud.

"Do you know what it means to call someone a cow?" The girl-woman's voice was not threatening, but got their attention.

"I'll tell you."

Micah wiped her nose with the back of her hand.

"It's saying you are strong. Gentle. Patient. And it's also saying, we don't really know *who* you are. You are a sweet mystery to me. Maybe a little scary. Boys often find girls a little scary."

Theo wondered whether this stranger was going too far with "her" kids. She was saying things people don't usually say. Of course a hamburger is dead cow. But it's not something you emphasize, especially to children. She was transgressing, and Theo assumed that's why she got both her and the children's attention. She was transgressing and yet she seemed safe, sane. Her beauty was reassuring.

Theo tried to collect the children and herd them onto the bus.

"Time to"—her words floated through the air—"go."

Then something happened. It was a small thing. Collecting children onto a bus. Shouting so they could hear. Like a child, it was small and immense at once. Theo took a deep breath and shouted, "Micah, Carlos, Christopher, Evan, Emily... it is TIME."

The children listened. Theo felt her voice carry the names of the children, and her mood shift.

The young woman stood nearby, watching.

"Tough job you have," she said.

Theo looked up at her, for she was considerably taller than Theo, at her large mouth, thin but strong shoulders, small breasts hugged by a tight brown T-shirt, long girlish arms dangling at her side, and of course her hair—a long, thick flame of orange framing her pale, freckled face.

"Dull, mostly. I'm not great with children."

"I know what you mean, I could never..."

"Yes you could; I saw how you handled them. Besides, you're still a kid yourself. You seem to like children. And cows."

"I *am* a cow." The girl smiled.

She said this matter-of-factly, with certainty, the way another woman might say, I am an attorney and I have three boys.

And it was clear she didn't mean it in the sense Theo's mother had used the words, as an utterance of exasperation, or self-hatred. *Ach, ich bin doch so eine blöde Kuh.* Oh, I am such a stupid cow.

Anyone with imagination can get under the skin of another being. This was what Theo heard, not then but later.

"You're an awfully skinny cow," Theo played along.

"Maybe you need your lens prescription changed," the girl, athletic-looking as Johanna, came back.

"So I can see the world through cow-tinted glasses."

"Sure."

Evan hesitated nearby before boarding the bus. He was the last and Theo had lost track of him. The girl gave him a pat on the head, bending to look him in the eye, and said, "You're a good kid."

This must have revved his engine, for he ran and then hopped up to the first step of the bus and, as soon as he'd found a seat, opened the window and began waving to his new friend.

About to board the bus herself, Theo tried for a moment to see her thirty-two-year-old face the way the girl might see it. Choices, too much wasted time, already etched there. Dark hair, milky skin. Blue eyes obscured and magnified at once by thick—cow-unfriendly—glasses. About eight inches taller, the girl would see her face from above, from an angle unknown to Theo.

"I'm Hazel." She stretched out a large hand. "Here, from the East Coast, visiting my father," she told Theo, who took Hazel's hand, its softness too intimate.

Visiting, Hazel said, rather than searching for. Could she have Theo's number? They might go for a walk sometime. Theo tore off a piece of an old attendance sheet and scribbled her number on the back of it.

"Your name?" Hazel asked.

"Theona." She used her full name, which, having died with her mother years ago, had grown unfamiliar.

*

At home that evening Theo took out her index cards and spread them on the small table that stood in front of the futon sofa. She was working sometimes enthusiastically, often ambivalently on this dissertation and had been at the beginning too long. Theo looked at the cards, scribbled with enthusiasms of the moment, willing them to give her a sign about where to place her focus. She could not seem to get beyond the vague, yet powerful, urge to write about loss. The cards were her attempt to formulate something more specific and workable:

Postwar Germany was perceived as a country unable to mourn.

The American housewife is the obverse of the cowboy; also solitary, but stationary. Does she achieve contentment by approaching her unchanging frontier each day as though for the first time, or by finding something new, not unlike Thoreau on his walks, in an always deepening intimacy with her familiar terrain?

What is it that breaks a child?

Suicide as a final attempt at development.

Don't write about anything too close to home, Theo's Advisor advised. But her definition of home was ill-defined at the time. Her interview with M was premature and unprofessional not only because she'd slept with him, but also because she had not yet developed a premise for the interview and the questions asked. Theo had run an ad offering to pay twenty-five dollars in exchange for 'assistance with psychological research.' It was the only way she could think of to get out of her own diffuse thoughts and, possibly, to move forward.

Since meeting M, Theo had written on additional cards: *immigrants and homesickness, changes of heart, sex and ambition, dangerous work, repetitive work, the attraction of the foreigner.* In this way, too, her meeting with M had been fruitful, though she decided not to do any more interviews until she had a coherent proposal. The serendipity of meeting Hazel, who seemed to have an unusual feeling about cows, just after her last encounter with M, was something she noted but did not spend much time thinking about.

Her pile of index cards was growing as high as the stack of postcards she'd received from Johanna the first year she was away. Theo kept both sets of cards in shoeboxes, the one holding Johanna's cards dating back to the time they both wore high-top sneakers, Johanna's two sizes larger, so they could never trade. This box of cards was somewhere in the closet, except for one card, which Theo kept on her wall. It was the last Johanna had sent, almost thirteen years ago.

This last card, which had faded a little, once symbolized for Theo a wrong turn, a kind of paralysis that she experienced but did not understand. For a long time, when she looked at it, it posed the question: Why didn't you go? It was a question she'd stopped asking herself, not because she had an answer, but because its importance had, like the card, faded.

The postcard depicted a street in the German village where their mother had lived when she was a young child. On the other side, Johanna had written, *I can't wait to see you!!!* And so Johanna's enthusiasm met Theo's inertia. Theo can still remember how all the exclamation marks overwhelmed her and that sometime later she turned them into a doodle of a porcupine.

Theo was nineteen at the time, living in her first apartment in a northeastern college town. It always seemed to be raining that fall, her first away from Johanna, their brother, and their father. Johanna had moved to Germany immediately after graduating from high school. Johanna— the rebellious and yet favored, who several colleges wanted for their tennis or basketball teams, or both.

You could get library privileges at the college, you know. The man who owned the bookstore had said this to Theo not long after she'd gotten what would be Johanna's last card. He said it in such a way that Theo somehow inferred an invitation—to what she was not sure, but an invitation. She spent too much time reading the books in his store without buying anything. Every day she walked over from the coffee shop where she worked and read the beginnings and sometimes the endings of novels. This was the extent of her reading. She was too anxious to read, to allow herself the time to read an entire book. Besides, the proper friction between eye and word was too often absent; her eyes had trouble holding the words long enough for meaning to settle.

The bookstore man told her he disliked all the spoiled college girls, that he could tell she was different, just naturally smart. (Theo would not begin college until years later, after she moved to California and established residency.) No one had said anything flattering to her in quite a while. It was a hook, and she felt lifted up.

Her sister's postcards crowded the sill, some always falling to the floor. After getting what would be the last card, the one showing a row of houses in their mother's village, Theo took them from the sill and pinned them to the wall, in the order in which she'd received them. She looked at the next to last card, a photo of Cologne at Carnival. A large float in the shape of a dragon took up most of the card. Riding the float, two men dressed as Nordic heroes threw candy to the crowds in the street. In the background, fragments of the blackened cathedral peeked through the wooden boards placed around it for the occasion. On the other side of the card, Johanna had written: *This is where Mom and Dad met . . . Soon you can see it for yourself! I miss you. I'm so excited that you might visit! Love Jo.*

Her sister, Theo knew, lived southwest of Cologne, in the city their mother had lived in during the last years of the war, until the family's apartment was bombed, at which time they sought refuge in the village depicted on that last card. Theo studied all the cards. There were postcards of the Rhine, of vineyards, of various German cities. This was her sister's life, as she was telling it to Theo. There were no long letters, no phone calls. A few days after Theo thought about going to see Johanna, she put the cards, except for the last one, away.

Theo could not say that she decided not to go, only that she did not go. She intended to go. A part of her had intended to go. They were sisters, after all. She had a little money in the bank. But why should she? She was just getting used to separation, to being alone.

Eventually, after way too much time had passed since she'd received Johanna's last card, Theo had written: *I'm not able to get away. Sorry. I can't really explain.*

She'd erased the last line and replaced it with, *I miss you, too.* Johanna did not answer at first, and then sent a package of tea and chocolates.

After studying the postcards for a long time that evening, when she was nineteen, Theo had taken a walk along the main street leading out of town. It was a drizzly evening. She'd been walking for about half an hour when she saw a porcupine sitting in the middle of the road. The animal stood on its hind legs and held its front paws together and slightly lifted off the road. It did not move as Theo approached, nor did it move for cars. Theo wondered whether it could be dead, but could not imagine any creature dying and staying in that position. She walked closer to it and saw that it was partly skinned along its spine. Red, pink, and white flesh was exposed, not bleeding, but raw with blood held on a surface about the size of two fists. Layers of skin and quills had slid down its side but were still attached by a small piece of skin. The porcupine was trembling, apparently unable to move. Theo felt she was looking at a creature on the very edge of death, in a near-death trance. She'd met a prickly Buddha, a little Jesus. She wanted to move it out of the way of cars but knew she couldn't.

She walked back to town to the bookstore, rehearsing how she would come on to the owner. It was so easy, in bed, to know how to move. She'd learned it all through high school and had been smart enough to keep it a wonderful secret from her family and from that house where pleasure had almost no place.

Theo and the bookstore owner's one night developed into a love affair and then a relationship lasting five years. Frank gave her a job at the bookstore and Theo moved in with him. She was able to save some money, and soon began making plans to go away to college. Theo had never thought that someone would or could help her, but he did. By the time she left for California, she knew she could read and think and have a relationship, and she did not care so much that he, one night, found someone else.

Theo scanned her cards. *The amnesiac is perhaps happiest; like an infant he or she travels light . . .*

She continued to take random notes on what interested her. At fifty-two, a full deck, she would stop and it would all come together. She'd had this thought, just a lark really. *You're not playing with a full deck.* Her father's words to her mother came back. Theo put the index cards away and went to the closet to look for the old shoebox that held Johanna's postcards.

*

After Theo's school bus left, Hazel returned to the animals. A desolate peace hung in the air, trailing the departed children's voices. The merry-go-round on the other side of the eucalyptus grove was silent. The fog had lifted and now it was bright, too bright for the number of hours she'd been awake. Only one other person was around, an elderly man sitting on a bench with a folded newspaper at his side. She observed the Holstein. Yes, she was well along in pregnancy. But she looked too old and haggard to birth. Maybe she was mistaken, and the bulge was something else. She certainly was no expert.

Hazel began rubbing one side of the cow's head. It was soft and warm. She put her face close to the cow's face and looked at the inside of her ear, still newborn pink behind the fine hairs.

She sat down on an empty bench and thought of her family. At twenty she had not had a relationship that could help her understand marriage. People can walk away from happiness as well as unhappiness, her mother said when Hazel dared to say: it seemed good between you. Her parents had often been affectionate, occasionally passionate, in her presence. She never doubted their love for each other. There was no divorce, and after a few years Hazel began to long for one—a reason, at least, for his not being with them.

She and her mother were living peacefully in the New York farmhouse where Petra had given birth to Hazel twenty years earlier. Mother and daughter shared the gift of adjusting gracefully to circumstance, of connecting tenaciously to place. No need to speak of longing and absence when the terrain is understood—where the well is, how deep it is, how much drought it has survived.

Walking back from the barn after putting the goat to bed, Hazel had stopped at the mailbox, and there it was. This should be written to Mom, too, she said to the black scrawl, to the fog, the bridge, to the open space, and the smell of another dusk without him.

On that August day five years ago, their last together, Hazel and her father sat close on the cooling sand, looking out over the bay to the opposite shore dotted with houses and camps. Her mother had gone further down the beach to gather stones, a sharp vertical figure in the distance, holding a large bucket. Hazel felt the familiar chill as the day wore thin; she reached for a long-sleeved cotton shirt that lay crumpled between her and her father. This was one of her favorite sensations—feeling the hot sun fade, getting that slight chill, then putting something on that retained the sun's heat. She imagined this was the kind of comfort her parents felt when they lit a cigarette outside on a cool evening.

No, he had said nothing of his plans. He was not a man who made plans. We are all tending a garden, he'd said to her once. A garden no one else and sometimes not even we ourselves can see. He was a sentimental man. He held onto vagueness, to mystery, the obfuscation of his own motives, the way another man might keep a gun.

Instead, he told her the story of Liam's accident. She had heard stories about her grandfather before, stories that alluded to an accident but never focused on it. Gabriel told and retold stories of his youth, spilling fragments, grasping at bits of things he almost remembered clearly, about his childhood in the Midwest, about his parents, their poverty and homesickness. More than once he had to do his school-work on butcher paper. He couldn't get the work right or was late, once again, to class and therefore denied real paper. I had to beg for it, he said. And the pencil never did show up right on it. He stopped going to school and wandered for miles to be free of the stench of the place where his parents lived and toiled, for you, they said, for your future.

Hazel met her grandfather just twice before he died. He was missing his right hand. She remembered the reddish stump, rounded and as smooth-looking as a baby's knee. It first frightened and then intrigued her. When Liam caught her looking at it he said nothing and looked away. She, too, looked away.

Liam and Nora had left Ireland for Chicago because Liam's uncle Jack had written, saying there were plenty of jobs where he was living. No one had thought to ask what kinds of jobs. Liam was twenty-three, and they had been moving from farm to farm as laborers for the last several years, Liam having, as the third son, inherited no land of his own. Nora did not want to leave Ireland. She was educated, had completed high school and training as a nurse. She could have gotten a job, but Liam would not hear of it. Just pregnant with Gabriel, she agreed they needed to look for a better life.

They arrived in 1938, latecomers, most of the Irish having arrived at the Chicago stockyards a generation or two before. Liam was given a job at the slaughterhouse, while Nora focused on her growing belly, the only thing around her that made any sense at all. She talked and sang to her child. She told him what she couldn't or wouldn't tell to anyone else. And she apologized for taking him away from the soil that had nourished and received again all prior generations of O'Connells and Doyles.

Fifteen years later, two years after he had been moved from his latest job to the kill floor, Liam lost his right hand when a cow bolted in one fierce, futile effort to save her life. She knocked Liam over, her weight forcing the knife he was holding in his left hand clear through the other.

"If they'd had money, if there were more decency in the world, his hand could have been saved," Gabriel said to Hazel that summer when she was fifteen and they sat on the beach.

When Liam died, Nora returned to Ireland almost immediately. She took his ashes with her and had him buried in the family cemetery. Now she lay beside him without having seen her son or granddaughter again. "Tell him to come," she had written Hazel. But Hazel had no way of passing on the message.

No grandparents alive and none buried near was its own kind of loneliness. Her father was the seedling Liam and Nora had brought with them. Their return to Ireland may have said to him this: you failed to take hold. You did not grow into anything worth staying for.

"Did you know he joined the union not long before the accident?"

Hazel did not know. She held a wet, blue gray stone, smooth and solid in her palm.

"It is what sent him down. The hope for something better and then the accident just after. Drove him to drinking. Nora saved him. They had a strong marriage, were crazy about each other. The O'Connells marry for love. That's important to remember, little faerie."

Gabriel threw a stone into the water. It skipped once and was swallowed. He turned toward his daughter and looked past her, a man accustomed to being looked at rather than looking. He was so beautiful, Nora said, the other boys used to tease him, calling him Gabriella. Once when he was about eight he cut his dark curls off with a pair of nail scissors, but even with the ragged tufts of hair he was too beautiful. And he was too tender for Chicago. It wasn't a place for any child. But at least, she said, he didn't drown in the gutter before he turned two, like Jurgis and Ona's child in *The Jungle*. Throughout her pregnancy Nora read that book. It was the story of their world.

"It wasn't that he had never killed before," Gabriel continued. "He had. You don't grow up on a farm in Ireland and not kill a pig once in a good year. But this was a factory of killing, like nothing he had ever seen. There came a day, it must have been early on, when he had to decide either to close his heart or quit." Gabriel looked at her briefly. "He did not quit," he said, "not until years later, after the accident, when he was forced to. Focusing like that on the same task over and over, day and night, could push any man into an agony of trance or madness. Like driving on a straight road for days, your mind is bound to wander. You are bound to get careless. And when it's throats you have to slit, not one throat, but hundreds a week, well, Mercy God. It's not like opening envelopes with a penknife."

Hazel remembered how her mother approached them with her bucket full of stones. She could see that the arthritis in her fingers was worse by the way her mother held the bucket, hugging it awkwardly to her chest rather than holding it by the handle. It was becoming more difficult to carve stone. Increasingly, she added to rather than took away from her material. Fascinated by its relation to textile, she went to garage sales and thrift stores looking for old clothing, fabric that caught her attention.

There had been no fight, no argument. No visible signs of the end of a marriage. They packed up and left the camp as scheduled. When they arrived home, Gabriel took his things out of the car, put them into his old pickup, and kept on driving to, presumably, the airport. The airport did call them weeks later asking about the abandoned truck. "I love you, little faerie," was all he had said to her, his almost six-foot-tall daughter.

*

"I'll be back," Hazel said to the Holstein and began walking out of the park, fingering the scrap of paper on which Theo had written her number. Strong whiffs of honeysuckle, rose, and lemon mingled with the cooling air. She quickened her pace, eager now to get back to the house.

The driveway was empty. The imitation Tudor exterior, the ornate rounded front door, loomed large and ridiculous, unlike anything she could imagine her father living in. Newspapers were scattered on the lawn. A few were tucked under the shrubs that surrounded the front yard. She sat down on the stoop and hung her head over her knees into the smell of boxwood and summer dusk.

"You should file a missing persons report," friends had said to her mother. "Anything could have happened."

"I will not. I know my husband," Hazel still heard her mother say.

"He was always a bit off. Just so quiet, and the way he laughed at things—like a child. Hear he could barely read or write."

"Don't pay them any attention." Carol, her mother's friend and the midwife who had helped deliver Hazel, said when Hazel went to her, only once, for comfort.

She got up and walked the narrow passageway between this and the neighboring house, around to the back. The burglar lights next door came on, then switched off. A lemon tree stood enclosed by a small fence, the fruits effervescent lights in the darkening. She walked over to it and turned to look up at the large French windows, which opened to a deck. My father could never afford a place like this, she thought again. This was the landscape of memory lapse. Yet she had checked the address several times, compared the number on the door repeatedly with that on the postcard. She felt a familiar queasiness spread through her middle and thought, I am standing in a stranger's backyard.

She walked up to the deck and looked in the window. It was too dark to see much. All she could make out were the vague shapes of furniture, which revealed nothing. When she turned around there was the view that the windows must have framed, a view not unlike that on his postcard, though now the contours of the Golden Gate Bridge were crisp and elegant against the clear night sky.

The brass knocker on the neighbor's door hung at eye level when Hazel stood one step down from the entrance. A woman, probably in her early forties, poked her head out, a child of about four holding onto her leg.

"I'm sorry to bother you," Hazel began. "I wanted to know if Gabriel O'Connell lives next door."

"We just moved in yesterday," the woman said. "I'm sorry I can't tell you anything."

The woman's phone started ringing, and she began moving toward it.

"I'm his daughter," Hazel ventured.

"Sorry." The woman smiled and closed the door.

Hazel stood there for a moment and then went back next door. She gathered all the stray newspapers and piled them neatly on the deck before walking away.

She walked out into the night, along the well-lit sidewalks, not knowing where she was going. Neither seemed real—the fact that she'd come all this way or the fact that he was not where he said he would be. There's been a mistake and it will be cleared up. He is not a cruel man. She had not bought a return ticket and now was not sure whether this had been an act of optimism or despair.

3

Hazel called Theo rather late, just as Theo was getting ready for bed.

"I need a place to stay tonight," she said. "It's Hazel."

Theo was startled by her directness. "What about your father?"

"He's not home."

"You mean you traveled three thousand miles to see him and he's not there?"

Hazel said nothing.

"Well, let's meet for coffee first," Theo said.

Theo put down the phone and lay back on her bed. On the wall behind the bookshelf, which held the phone, was the last postcard from Johanna. She'd tacked it up mostly out of habit, but for some reason had actually been looking at it when Hazel called. The house in the foreground was white stucco, with a clay-shingled roof bright orange in sunlight. Purple flowers climbed a garden wall and the front corner of an adjacent building that could have been a stable. The picture was taken from above, but not from very high up. From another rooftop maybe, or a tree. She liked to imagine someone, perhaps a child, sitting in a tree, snapping the photo.

Theo was too tired to go out but did not want to invite Hazel over without meeting her again first. She imagined Hazel saying her name. Theona. Why had she introduced herself that way? Theona looks like a French intellectual, like a woman too susceptible to love. She smells faintly of cigarettes, but not like a heavy smoker. She can stretch her money. The thrift shop clothes are just right, always. And the ring with the green stone, the only jewelry she wears, it is curious. No. Hazel would not think any of this. A woman who had to fight her way out of something, maybe.

Maybe she would see that. A wily animal just on the verge of discovering, slowly and all at once, that she might survive. No. An older woman. A place to stay for the night.

"Twenty is a scrunched photograph," Theo said when Hazel told her she'd just had a birthday.

They had agreed to meet at a trendy deli not far from where Hazel had called.

"It couldn't have been that long ago," Hazel smiled. "What were you doing then?"

Theo found she wanted to give a perfect confession or, at least an entertaining anecdote, but nothing came.

"I don't remember."

Hazel was drinking soda water, Theo coffee with lots of cream. They both wore the same clothes they had on earlier, and this seemed odd to Theo because the context was now so different. Sitting across from Hazel, for a moment she sees Johanna, tall and lovely like Hazel but blond. She sees Johanna turning toward her once more before walking through the security gate to board her flight. Johanna waves with her free hand and smiles. "What about your sports scholarships?" Theo had asked as they sat on their parallel twin beds late at night, the night before Johanna was to leave, only three nights after her high school graduation. Their father and brother had surely been asleep. "I don't know," Johanna said. In the glaring airport light, the sisters wave to each other, change into other people.

"I hope you like cats as much as you like cows." Theo's invitation to Hazel. "I have a cat."

Theo had found Job (pronounced with a short *o*) in a dumpster. As she was lifting her week's worth of garbage she heard his cry, so loud she expected a huge creature, not a kitten the size of her hand. She'd posted a sign in the courtyard and along the street: *Found Kitten*. Afraid of provoking the guilty person's ire, she did not write where she'd discovered him. Nobody called and she, of course, did not expect anyone to. She just wanted it known that he was in the world and that someone knew about it. The sign was, in its own way, like a birth announcement.

He was a mess, but he pulled through. She took him home from the vet and nursed him into a robust and confident kitten. He became her companion and gave her the invaluable gift of someone to think about other than herself. Putting out her garbage was never the same again. Each time she approached the smelly metal container that stood at the back of her apartment building she heard that cry and expected to find Job again, in another form perhaps, but with the same cry.

"I love cats. I have one at home." Hazel stared at Theo's coffee.

"What is it?" Theo asked.

"Nothing."

"So—you need a place to stay. Didn't your father leave a key?"

Hazel looked down at her fingernails, which were cut, or perhaps bitten, very short. "No. If you don't want me to stay at your place, you could help me break in."

"Now I like that idea." Theo laughed.

"Actually, I'm not sure I have the right house."

"Then it would be a bad idea."

Theo was still chuckling, when she noticed Hazel's expression had gone sad and tired.

"You've been up a long time," Theo said, noticing again that she was also very tired and that the coffee was making her nauseous.

"I'm worried about my father." Hazel's voice was soft and high-pitched, like a young child's.

Theo could not know what it cost Hazel to say this. And yet she sensed it, the understatement of the strong and very vulnerable. It was a confession long in coming, given by someone not prone to confession.

Theo remembered her own father and the time she was putting away a warm, soft pile of his handkerchiefs that her mother had just ironed. She'd opened the top drawer of the oak dresser he shared with Theo's mother and jumped back when she saw a revolver lying next to his underwear. It lay there casually like loose change. Theo never mentioned it, fearing this in itself could make it go off. As a child it had occurred to her, once she understood how babies were made, that she had the war, and by extension the Nazis, to thank for her existence. Her father had been one of the American soldiers who stayed in the decades following the war. Her parents met near the devastated Cologne Cathedral. Theo's mother agreed to marry the American but never forgave him for bombing her city, the city where she'd spent what she once referred to as her best years, as a music student.

Theo was hungry suddenly and ordered a roast beef sandwich.

Hazel, grateful for Theo's company, said nothing. She had generally been one to stay quiet, to observe and stay quiet, and she would stay quiet now, for now. This was best. In the long run it hurt least. Yet she had never traveled this far alone before, had never missed this much sleep, and she had certainly never gone looking for her father. These things, and the different air and perhaps something about Theo began to unravel, if not Hazel herself, then something intricate and well-wrought Hazel had crafted around herself. She had been used to putting her hopes and fears to bed each night carefully, making sure they slept soundly and disturbed no one; now she felt they'd been forced awake, and together they stood on a precipice. From this precipice she allowed herself, instead of talking to Theo, a few words to the cows. No one heard those words. They were a sharp little breeze wrapped in the now fragile calyx of Hazel's silence.

"I'll have a tempeh sandwich," Hazel said to the waitress.

"Was he expecting you?"

Hazel could not answer this. It seemed the wrong question, just as all questions regarding her father had always seemed wrong.

They ate for a while in silence. Theo was amused when she remembered that Hazel had called herself a cow, and now here she was eating a roast beef sandwich.

"Where do you live?" Hazel asked.

"In the flats. A long way from here, but we can walk."

*

Like her father, Hazel was an only child, and when she was very young she had often conjured an imaginary sibling. This sister or brother—she had imagined both—she loved perfectly; they were inseparable and exactly the same age. This twin was the one person in the world from whom she did not need to protect herself.

It was past midnight and she had traveled across the country on what now seemed a rash impulse, but she felt suddenly happy. Her father was no closer or farther than he'd ever been. The air was so sweet. Even the smell of Theo's cigarette was sweet. If you didn't think ahead (or about the horrors) but just noticed what was around you, things were generally good. She liked Theo. There was something reckless, backward, and yet aware about her.

Theo knew something, and what she didn't know kept her young. No, they were not so far apart.

They passed garden after garden, the landscaping getting simpler, then absent altogether, as they came down from the hills. She was moving away from him, from his phantom house and the possibility of his hands having dug dirt and planted. By the time they reached Theo's apartment there was only sidewalk and brown grass. A man lay under a car fixing something. Tools were spread out on the sidewalk beside a lit flashlight, which they had to walk around.

Walking through the courtyard of her apartment building earlier, on her way to meet Hazel, Theo had passed two women hammering in the dark. They were making a sandbox, which was now completed, a few shovels and buckets already thrown in, though there was no sand yet. Theo thought of the sleeping children, of their laughter and the chatter that rose to her window the mornings she worked at home, and imagined their glee at discovering their world improved.

"I had one," Hazel broke their long silence, "made of a circle of stones just outside my mother's studio."

"Mine was wooden," Theo said. "I think my father made it. Just four boards nailed in a square." Theo and Johanna would take turns burying each other. They made gardens in the sand, from sticks and leaves they tore off trees. Whole afternoons passed in that box. And then came that feeling, of being suddenly too big, wrists and ankles and time hanging awkwardly.

"I love letting the warm, soft sand run through my fingers." Hazel thought of her sandbox and of the beach in Maine. "I tried washing my hair with sand once; a dry wash is good for hair."

Job sidled up to Hazel as she walked through the door. "Job," Hazel said, and bent down to pet him. He followed her down Theo's narrow hallway, his brown and white mottled haunches full of purpose.

Theo did not want to turn on the fluorescent light, but there was no other until the living room on the far side of the kitchen. She had forgotten what a barren mess her place was. A dirty glass stood next to an unused candle on the card table. The one kitchen chair was pushed out into the middle of the room like a stage prop. There were dirty dishes in the sink, evidence of several solitary meals. The whole kitchen reflected a stiff, forlorn untidiness that felt suddenly repulsive to her. She was sure Hazel would one day build herself a carefully put-together and maintained nest.

"Sorry about the mess," she said unimaginatively. "Let's just go through to the living room."

Hazel sat down on the sofa, and Job immediately hopped onto her lap.

"He doesn't do that with everyone, you know. That's your bed. Would you like a beer?"

"Do you have any tea?"

Theo rolled her eyes. "I don't allow people without vices to sleep over at my place. Name me one, just one, and I'll make you some tea, if I can find some."

Hazel smiled, her eyes almost closing.

Theo went back into the kitchen and opened a cabinet door. In a back corner behind an old bag of lima beans, dating from a period in which she had vowed to make herself large quantities of homemade soup, she found the unopened tin of chamomile tea. Johanna had sent the tea along with some chocolate about six months after Theo failed to visit. Theo could have understood the package as a sign of forgiveness if there had been a note. But there were no words then or since then. Theo had eaten the chocolates immediately. She wanted to find her sister in each bite, hoping crazily for a note stuck into the center of one. When she opened the neatly wrapped package that contained the tea tin, which had drawings of various flowers on it, again with no note, she thought, we will drink this tea together someday. And then she put it away.

"Thank you," Hazel said. Theo handed her the tea and sat down with her beer on the rocker. "It smells good." She took the mug with both hands. They were large hands, with long, strong fingers, prominent joints. Theo was feeling jittery and queasy. Too much coffee or a stomach bug, she thought. She held her bottle of beer.

"It's late." Theo felt she wanted to lie down and sleep.

"I'm not tired anymore," Hazel said like a child resisting bed.

"You're exhausted. You must be. It's three in the morning Eastern Time."

Hazel looked at the small bookshelf behind Theo lined with books from all her courses.

"So you're going to become a shrink?"

"Oh, no. After I unlock the secret of the human psyche I'm going to retire to Florida."

Hazel giggled. "Seriously, what are you going to do? I mean, why are you studying psychology? You're going to become a shrink, aren't you? Or study rats?"

"I don't know. I just wanted to figure something out."

"And did you?" Hazel looked her in the eye with an openness she could not remember having seen before in anyone.

"No." Theo closed her eyes and there was her mother, standing on their square of suburban lawn, her young children asleep inside the house. She is staring at the silhouettes of the house across the street, the large spruce tree, the small dogwood, the fire hydrant, cars parked in driveways. Birds sing their hearts out, but the hush is louder, the hush of families with such separate lives, the hush of the universe moving away from her.

This is one of a stockpile of images Theo had come to years ago when she tried to imagine her mother at the moment of deciding.

Hazel took her pennywhistle out of her back pocket and began to play softly. Theo looked at her, at her open face, her generous features framed by the striking hair. Then she leaned back and closed her eyes again. She must have drifted off because when she came to, Hazel was curled on the sofa, asleep, with Job lying by her feet. Theo got up and found Hazel's sleeping bag, covered her, and stumbled into the bedroom.

*

The next morning, early, Hazel walked the long walk back to the house. One more paper had been tossed on the lawn. Hazel took the newspaper out of its plastic bag and opened to the want ads. She had no money and would need to find a job, one she could walk to. She sat on the stoop again, inhaling the smell of boxwood. It smelled like the garden in Germany where her mother had taken her when, Hazel believed, she decided Gabriel would not be coming back. "I want to show you," she said, "where my parents met and fell in love." They stood together in a cobblestone courtyard beside a limestone fountain and watched large goldfish swim in circles. "I can imagine a wedding here," Hazel reassured her mother, who had lost those two wedded people at age five.

Hazel noticed an ad for work at a juice bar. She had seen the place on her walk. She folded the newspaper and stacked it with the others. A man was squeezing oranges when she walked in. "You can start now." He tossed her an orange, smiling. Hazel caught it. "OK." She worked until six that evening and then walked back up to the park to visit the Holstein. The farm would be closed, but she wanted to go anyway.

Theirs would be a brief acquaintance. Hazel knew the cow was in trouble. All the animals were inside the barns. It was very quiet for a while, except for birdsong and the occasional car carrying late park visitors. She was wondering what Theo would say when she asked to stay another night, when the lowing began. It was soft, grew louder. Then it faded again. It didn't sound ordinary. She had never heard a cow in labor. Could it be starting already? She didn't think so.

The cow is sacred in India, but what does that mean? She thought of the buffalo, sacred and vital to the Native American and therefore eradicated. For Hazel it was not one animal over any other, though it was the cow to whom she had chosen, most often, to speak. Her grandfather was a killer of cows and that, she felt, brought her into a special relation with this particular animal. After speaking to cows Hazel felt empty and peaceful, as though having marched through the worst. This was a trick she had begun during her father's last and apparently permanent absence. When pain came too close and too strong she thought of the dark place to which he had introduced her. She thought of the abattoir. And her life, her relative freedom, rained down on her its golden rain and, now, the words: Do Something.

4

Hazel returned to Theo's that evening with a five-pound bag of dust-free sand.

"For the box. Unless you want it for your hair."

"What's next in terms of looking for your father? Is it the wrong house or not?"

Hazel shrugged. "I found a job. Worked most of the day."

"You can stay if you like, you know. For a little while."

Hazel was easy to live with, neat and not home too much. Besides, Theo, while she did not always enjoy it, needed the company. Hazel went to work and walked her route, stacking newspapers and visiting the cow. When summer and her camp job ended Theo spent long hours at the library and at home in front of her computer, still not sure exactly what it was she was researching. Three weeks went by and the stomach bug feeling only got worse. She was tired almost all the time. And then she knew.

Theo stared at the thin red line, first afraid that it wouldn't and then, decisively, that it would, disappear. Do not read results after ten minutes, the instructions said. After eating crackers and yogurt (she usually hated yogurt and this was her strongest clue that, yes, something had positively changed) she finally put the test in her underwear drawer, taking one last look at the line that meant the difference between baby and no baby. Then she made herself a cup of chamomile tea.

"The cow is in trouble." Hazel called just after Theo turned off her computer to lie down on the sofa. It was not yet nine o'clock, but she was exhausted. Never had it felt so good to lie down and do nothing. She was pregnant, busy enough.

"Throw some clean blankets or rags into your car and some water, a bottle if you have it, or pick one up at the drugstore, and come."

"What's going on?"

"Just come. I think the cow is calving."

"You should be calling a vet, not me."

"I know. I will. Please come."

The cow was in her stall hitting the back wall in her effort to get comfortable. She needed more room. Hazel unhooked the chain and led the cow out of the barn. The other cows started to low, out of sympathy or aggravation, Theo didn't know which. Hazel spread some straw for a bed. The cow's spine looked like it would tear through her skin. Her swollen abdomen heaved once, and then water rushed out of her, like when a water balloon pops. Theo stood back, but was close enough to see the calf inside its mother moving, like a kidnap victim in a tight bag. Hazel stroked the cow and whispered to her. Theo heard the clink-clank of chains, the restlessness of the others. A siren amplified, then faded. For a brief instant everything was still.

Hazel got out of the way. The forefeet emerged first, the right and then the left. The cow was still for a while, and then another contraction sent out the head and the entire length of the forelegs. Then it wasn't clear what came first, the cow's final push that sent her calf tumbling like a bundle of soft, wet loam into the straw, or her last breath. They came so close together. Hazel tried to bring her back, pushing down on her chest, looking for heart and lungs in the immense, motionless animal.

Theo was sweating. She had been here before.

The ambulance came for her mother just as it would for a person who still had a chance. Theo had dialed the numbers 9-1-1 and believed for those moments more surely in a miracle than ever before or since. The emergency medics went through procedures they probably knew were futile. Theo lay face-down on the gray living room carpet, willing with fists for her mother to take a breath. She herself did not appear to be breathing. Her father was around somewhere, her siblings absent, spared. She lay still.

The cow lay on her side. Her tongue hung out, her head nestled nicely in the straw. Flies buzzed around both mother and child. Hazel closed the staring eyes. Theo kept looking for breath, the way she did at the movies and the way she couldn't that night when she was fifteen. The little one, all extremities, was lying between her mother's legs, nuzzling, grabbing the lifeless but full teats.

After a few tries, the vet was able to get the calf to drink colostrum from a nipple. Theo still had the items she'd brought at Hazel's request in her car, and she felt foolish now for rushing around the drugstore, looking for a baby bottle.

The vet stroked and cleaned the calf vigorously. When Hazel tried to help, he said it would be best if she did not touch the animal. Legs looking as fragile as a heron's, it stood up, wobbled, and folded to the straw again. The second time its legs locked, then straightened. There it stood, looking around.

"It has an excellent chance of pulling through," the vet said.

"The calf is female, I think," Hazel said.

"Yes, that's right," the vet replied.

"Thank you for notifying us." The park service official sounded eager to get home.

"What will happen to them?" Hazel asked.

"We'll have the carcass picked up. The calf should stay at the clinic for a while, until she stabilizes."

"I'd like to buy them both from you," Hazel said.

Had she really said that? They all looked at her. What was she thinking?

"That cow needs to be moved before we open tomorrow morning. We have someone who handles these things."

"What if that person were to move her, and I would pay? I know where I want the cow taken." Hazel was on the mailing list of several animal advocacy organizations and had learned of a network of farms that rescued animals, mostly from factory farms.

"I think we need to know what you plan on doing with a dead cow, young lady."

"I want to take Patch to a farm and have her buried there and to bring Dusk there as well." She had named them. They were hers now, hers to free.

The man, exasperated, looked at Hazel and Theo and then over to the vet. Theo stepped back. Really, she hardly knew Hazel.

Theo imagined the phone call the man was making might be to the police. She stepped even further back toward the parking lot and her car. More words were exchanged. Theo caught only fragments. Something about dollars and beef. Something about trouble.

*

The cow had carried her calf for approximately nine and a half months. Theo thought about Patch and then tried to get her out of her mind. She did not want to be thinking about dying in childbirth. In fact she tried to minimize negative thoughts because she believed they would make her baby vulnerable to misfortune. She did yoga, focused on her breath. Despite her efforts, however, all through pregnancy ghosts flew in and out of her, like kites with long, knotted tails. Sometimes when they came she imagined the kite's string held in the translucent hand of a fetus.

Driving home from the park she told Hazel. "I'm pregnant."

"How?" Hazel asked, and they both laughed.

She had not seen M since the fateful night, though she tried to call. His roommate answered the phone and said M had moved back to Mexico. There'd been a raid on illegal immigrants. "There's no message," she said, as though she'd been given the choice of leaving one, and hung up.

Theo did not go along when Hazel borrowed Theo's car and followed the truck that carried the dead Holstein to the farm. Morning sickness, which presented itself at all hours, and the unfamiliar exhaustion of early pregnancy made driving one-hundred-and-fifty miles to bury a cow seem like a very bad idea. What kind of a farm, Theo wondered, would take a dead cow?

Hazel explained that this was not a farm that raised animals so they could be turned into food. This farm rescued a few animals and let them live their lives until they died a more or less natural death. The animals also served as mascots in the effort to educate the public about factory farming and slaughter. They would welcome Patch; they would believe she needed to be with her child, even in death.

In fact, when Hazel had called the farm, they had at first thought she was making a prank call. No, they said. We have enough trouble caring for live animals. Only when Hazel agreed to cover expenses and make a contribution did they agree. Hazel had never asked her mother for money before but was confident that she, too, would agree.

Theo was curious about this farm. It seemed like one of those dreams that was too good, just a little off, so that even while you were dreaming, you knew you'd have to wake up and face sharp, real morning. So she did agree to accompany Hazel when, after seven expensive days at the veterinary clinic, Dusk was ready to move.

"Think of all the money I've saved living at home and commuting to school. The money I'm asking for would not pay a month's rent in New York City. Well, not two months."

Theo listened to Hazel talking with her mother on the phone.

"Yes, Mom, I will. Definitely pay it back. You're saving one life, you know, and honoring another."

"No," Hazel's voice became quieter, less animated. "I don't know where he is. Yet."

To have one's mother at the other end of the line. For years, Theo had willed herself not to think about it. She sank a little deeper into the sofa and when Hazel hung up the phone pretended to be asleep.

Hazel sat down next to her, not fooled. "What is it?"

"Nothing." She could not say it, could not begin a sentence with the words "my mother."

"So she's going to give you the money," Theo said instead.

"She's going to loan it to me."

"Is she loaded, guilty, or just nice?"

"Just nice," Hazel answered, though she sometimes wondered whether her mother felt some guilt for choosing a man who left them.

"Are your parents still together?" Hazel asked.

"Never were. They barely spoke the same language." Theo's father felt no need to learn German, and her mother's English remained rudimentary. Learning English would have been, for her, a concession too big to make. Foreignness and incomprehension were her only weapons.

They rented a small horse trailer and hooked it to Theo's car, stopping every half-hour to check on Dusk.

"Slow down," Hazel said.

Theo was not in the best of moods, and ignored Hazel's request. She wasn't sure Hazel was old enough to legally pull a trailer, so she was stuck with the driving. She'd already used one of their rest stops to vomit.

Theo returned from the bathrooms to find Dusk sucking Hazel's finger. After a minute, Hazel replaced her finger with a bottle. When Dusk had finished drinking, Theo touched her for the first time. She stroked her nose, face, and black-spotted side, which was thin and not yet curved like the barrel on the typical adult cow. Barrel, pasterns, pinbone . . . Theo would learn the anatomy of the cow from Hazel. Dusk's mother was dead, and yet Dusk was lucky. She and Hazel had found each other, and now she would lead a charmed life on this farm, which Theo still had a difficult time picturing.

Aside from Job, Theo did not know many animals. Living in a city or suburb it was so easy to forget about them. There had been a series of cats at home when she was growing up, but they stayed outside because her mother was allergic. Yet her mother liked cats. It was she who brought them home. She aspired, Theo believed, to their reputed aloofness and independence.

Theo didn't know whether it was the first time or just the first time she remembered. Her mother said to her, "I burnt myself on the stove. I'm all right. Don't look at me that way, Theona."

Theo was five or six. Her sister had just started nursery school. Her brother not yet born. Their mother was alone in the house, moving as though her feet might leave the ground. She moved from room to room, a sleepwalker through a museum.

And there was another time, a few years later, when Theo was about ten, and her mother said, "I put my hand through a window, silly me."

"Where is it?" Theo had asked.

"What?"

"The broken window. Where is it?"

"I had it replaced, of course."

Screams come up through the heating vents sometime in the middle of the night. Theo gets up and puts the large picture encyclopedia she has come to use for this purpose over the opening. The voices muffle, but she cannot go back to sleep.

"This toast is burnt." Her father, the next morning.

"It's not burnt, it's just dark, Daddy." Johanna.

"I'm going to get a decent breakfast."

"Next time make your own goddamn toast." Their mother, to the screen door that never quite shut—that could never be slammed effectively.

There is something Theo is sure she is supposed to do. She is the oldest. Her insides are a cracked plate. Her little brother is crying. She stares down into her cereal bowl until she hears the school bus.

Later that day, her mother has bandages over her wrist and hand, but Theo doesn't see it right away. A neighbor has picked Theo and her siblings up from school and taken them to her house to play with her children.

"Your mother has had a little accident. She's OK. Don't worry."

They're shuffled into a large brown car. It smells of smoke. So does the house. Her parents only smoke outside. Theo does not want to play.

"You be the mother," the neighbor's eight-year-old girl says to Theo.

"I'll be the daddy," Theo's brother, Martin, says. Theo gives him a hug. They love each other best.

They all begin jumping on the large bed in the room. This is the "house." It is squeaky and springy, not like their homemade wooden beds.

"Children, children, listen to me." With a shy earnestness that she would never quite learn either bored others or made them uncomfortable, she begins to play.

Why does she want them to listen? Think of something. What would a mother say?

"We are going on a special trip today."

"Where, where, Mommy?" they all shout at once—Johanna, the other girl, and her two brothers. She has their attention. Now what?

They do not notice her silence.

"Disneyland, the circus, the zoo," they shout, jumping harder and faster until it sounds like the bed will break and Theo becomes frightened Martin will be bounced off on his head.

Five little monkeys jumping on the bed, one fell off and bumped his head. Four little monkeys . . . Theo sings and suddenly feels better.

They come home at dinner time, at what must have been dinner time, for they are hungry, but there are no smells of cooking.

"Where is it? Where is the window?" Theo insists.

"I had it replaced, of course. While you were gone." She is smiling. But not the good smile; the other one. The one connected to nothing.

"Which one?"

She looks at Theo.

"Which one was it? Which window?"

58

Theo looks out the dining room window that her mother points to and at the yew bush that divides their front yard from the neighbor's yard. All the children like to pick the berries and squish out the mucous insides, preferably on each other's clothes. The bush, its squat untrimmed shape, holds her in place.

"You're always so serious, Theona," her mother says. It is said without humor, an accusation. Her focus on the window, on the bush, tightens into a blur. It is impossible to ask, "How much does it hurt, Mommy?"

The farm was up on a rise, the hills summer brown. They parked at the end of a long gravel road in front of a small, white house that said, "office." It was getting very hot. A young woman about Hazel's age opened the door and approached them. Hazel waved, hopped out of the car and immediately went to open Dusk's trailer. Theo followed, looking around, a little dizzy with the heat. It was September, and eight years of living in California had not changed her sense that the leaves should be turning now.

Dusk lay in the bed Hazel had made for her in one corner of the trailer. Her long hind legs hung over the edge of the straw. She opened her brown eyes but did not stand.

"What's the matter with her?" Theo asked.

"She's just resting, getting used to being still."

"Best to drive her over to the barn," the young woman said.

They got back into the car and drove the short distance to the barn Dusk would have to herself until she was ready to join the others. When they opened her door, again she did not get up. Hazel got in and sat next to her, stroking her and humming. Theo stood with the other woman, who introduced herself as Lee. After a few more minutes Dusk got up. Hazel guided her out of the trailer and to pasture.

"She'll be fine," Lee said. Dusk began to chew a little grass. She stayed close to Hazel.

"Fine," Hazel repeated to Dusk, then kissed her above the nose and walked away.

"I have work to do," Lee said. "But you're free to look around."

The goats followed Theo while the sheep, with the exception of one, moved away. Theo sat down on a straw bale. The lone sheep stood about two feet from Theo's face and stared. A ram, Theo guessed. He had an apple-size growth bulging from his neck and a hairdo like Louis XVI. Theo learned later that this ram, like Job as a kitten, had been discarded. Near death, he was thrown onto a pile of dead animals at the stockyards. This was a common story, no one, apparently, taking a close enough look to distinguish between the dying and the already dead. But Theo did not know this as she sat returning the gaze of the ram. An unusual peace was upon her, as though she were in some kind of holding pen herself, temporarily separated from harm.

Most of the pigs were lying outdoors, sunning themselves or keeping cool in the mud. One hobbled toward Hazel when she held out an apple.

"They're bred to gain a lot of body weight very quickly," Hazel told her. "It's not long before their legs are too weak to carry them without trouble."

"Then isn't it merciful to kill them sooner?"

"That's the wrong question," Hazel snapped.

The pig grabbed the apple, chewing it loudly with the most crooked teeth Theo had ever seen. Only the pig's ears evoked the storybook kind of pig with a name and that you are supposed to love. Theo tried to conjure a voice reading to her about such a pig but couldn't. She remembered a voice coming from a record, but it was a chicken's voice. The sky is falling, it said.

There were three horses. Hazel referred to them as the pharmaceutical mares. They had been impregnated as often as possible and their estrogen-rich urine collected to produce a menopause drug. "The foals are by-products," Hazel said. "Maybe they'll come in handy, maybe they'll end up in the spare parts bucket." Theo walked away, to the turkey barn. The birds approached her immediately, leading with their ridiculously large breasts and clipped beaks. When she stroked their breasts they sat down as if among an old friend. It was gratifying at first but ultimately awkward, suggesting obviously misplaced trust.

Back at the office, Lee asked Hazel to fill out paperwork on Dusk.

"Let's watch some videos," Hazel said when she had finished. "You might learn something for your research."

"This has nothing to do with my research." She was angered by Hazel's statement, especially as she still had such a tenuous grasp on what it was she was researching.

Theo did not want to watch, and yet she was fascinated. She looked and then looked away and then looked again at the gloved hands slitting throat after throat, so efficiently, using the same motion again and again. Such a small movement was needed to end a life. The first video was taken undercover at a chicken and turkey slaughterhouse, the second at a cattle stockyard. For how many seconds can she watch birds hanging upside down, some still kicking, moving on a conveyor belt to the scalding vat? She thought of M. The camera lingers for too long on a dying calf atop a pile of dead animals. It records a spasm in the leg and the unmoving body parts of the surrounding carcasses. It records chains and a tractor that drag a downed cow to an awaiting truck, workers who prod and kick her, angry with her for causing them extra work, for reminding them of something they didn't want to be reminded of, for threatening to die before she brings a price.

"I want to show you where Patch is buried," Hazel said when they were outside again.

Theo grabbed some crackers from the car and followed Hazel up a hill to the far end of the pastures. Several giant cows were grazing. Not far from an apple tree was a bald section of earth about ten feet square.

"There she is." Hazel said this as if they were looking right at the old cow.

They stood on the freshly cut grass at the edge of the grave.

The grass she and Johanna did cartwheels on as children smelled like this, the lawn where their mother once, shortly after Martin was born, let them have a picnic with real china and cloth napkins.

"Thanks for coming with me," Hazel whispered, taking Theo's hand.

They moved to the apple tree and sat in the shade.

Even in the shade, the heat closed around her. Theo felt the shortness of breath she had read about. But that should come later, shouldn't it? Impatient, she often read ahead to descriptions of the more advanced months. It made her nervous, the thought that her child was smaller still than a sparrow. She shivered in the heat and withdrew her hand, close to tears. She did not want to cry in front of Hazel, fearing Hazel would take it to mean she wanted something. It's only hormones. Theo had read about that, too. This was as close as she could come to comforting herself.

They sat in silence interrupted only by the occasional animal or car sound.

Theo remembered *Charlotte's Web*. Extreme compassion for animals was something that, like Fern, one was supposed to outgrow. One moved on to other things, boys and Ferris wheels—if she remembered correctly. Watching the videos angered her. Helpless victims were not interesting. But the people connected to those gloved hands, these she could study—the living, struggling workers.

"Let's go dancing tonight," Hazel said, abruptly. "It will be good for the baby. And for you."

Theo hated it when someone told her what would be good for her. She hated it because she too often unwittingly accepted another's evaluation of her needs.

"You go. I'm not in the mood."

The long, hot afternoon stretched before them. When they returned to the city it would not yet be half over. The empty trailer bumped along the gravel road and away from the farm.

"We could stop somewhere for lunch," Hazel suggested.

"No, I want to get home," Theo said. She had an interview and her first appointment with the obstetrician scheduled for the next day.

Coming home together, and in the middle of the day, hadn't really happened before. When they walked down the hallway and into the kitchen of Theo's apartment, it felt like they had been gone a long time. It was refreshingly dark and cool inside.

Theo stood in her kitchen and watched Hazel stroke Job.

"Hungry?"

"Thirsty."

Theo poured two tall glasses of water.

She didn't feel like working. It came to her that what she longed for was desire itself. She longed for its focus and the reliable sense of deprivation that followed. Hazel, Job, the scrubby yellow kitchen floor, the white cabinets—how was she to place herself among them? She missed M. Perhaps they could have been happy together, over time.

Theo's exhaustion took over again like a wave she wanted only to ride into bed. As she peeled off her leggings, which she shouldn't have been wearing in the first place on such a hot day, she heard her mother's voice calling her children in to dinner just like the other mothers in the neighborhood. She looked at the worn stuffed lion from childhood on her pillow. She'd dragged it thus far through her life. In it, she liked to think, were all the good memories, or if not that, then at least the hope of childhood. When she lay down with her unborn child inside her, she knew all directions had disappeared. There was no other bed, no other room, and no one calling her home.

She woke to the sound of Hazel in the kitchen. The smell of oil and spices made her gag. She kept her eyes closed for a while, and when she opened them saw the late afternoon sun patterning the wall. She twisted the ring on her finger and then looked at the green stone, moving it until it caught the sunlight. It was not her mother's wedding ring. Her father had taken that. She can still see him throwing it across the room and then retrieving it, putting it in his mouth, weeping. "He loves you all," their mother had sometimes said after he'd lost his temper. "In his way."

No, this ring had belonged to her mother's mother, Theo's Oma. Theo's mother had the ring on when she died. "You're the oldest; you take it," her father ordered. For years, Theo kept it in a box with other jewelry she didn't wear. And then one day, not long ago, she put it on.

Dreams came immediately of taking it off and trying to give it to someone else. The someone else always either refused or vanished before the transaction was completed. She referred to this someone as the anonymous figure of longing, because the dream was always accompanied by a strong sense of longing, of a wish almost but never fulfilled.

Lies

5

Hazel often went to clubs alone or with friends in New York, and what she enjoyed most, aside from the dancing, was the labyrinthine sense of enclosure that the combination of lighting, moving bodies, and music produced. Dancing, she sometimes closed her eyes and imagined the way out hung by a thread to a dream she had not yet had. She danced with a natural grace and rhythm and, tonight, with an intensity that created a circle around her. She enjoyed possessing this space, and then losing it by weaving through people to find yet another opening. This was her pleasure for a while, until she felt a sudden disconnection both from the music and her own movements. She bumped into several people and apologized. She was experiencing a sensation unfamiliar to her—a desire to run from an inner discomfort that propelled her forward too quickly.

She left the dance floor, sat down at the bar, and ordered a soda water. A young man about her age sat down next to her and ordered a beer.

"You're quite a dancer."

Hazel fingered and began to peel the label on her club soda bottle.

"What do you want to do with your life?" Hazel asked him.

"Not much of a small talker, are you?"

He told her he worked at a photocopy place and was taking a few night classes in computer graphics.

Hazel stared at the array of liquor bottles across from her. They were colorful, brightening with whatever light came their way. The man behind the bar looked at her and winked.

"I mean, what do you want to do to make the world a better place? If we don't," Hazel went on, "there's not going to be a livable world very much longer."

"You were more fun when you were dancing." He looked at her and continued in a tone of self-mockery, "I can copy propaganda for you, or a love letter, it doesn't matter. As many as you like, all of them the same, I get paid the same. Let's dance."

The music was good. She loved moving to it.

"Come home with me," he said, drawing her toward him. "I have my own place."

Come home with me, come home with me—she imagined the words printed, as they had been spoken, endless times, with endless variations of inflection, expressing the same longing.

He was good looking, with curly dark blond hair and intelligent eyes, but she had no interest.

Hazel sometimes thought about getting an apartment in New York City, where she was studying. But it was so expensive, and the truth was she enjoyed living at home with her mother. She loved the old farmhouse, her room, and the fields and woods that surrounded their house. The safety and the quiet of the mosses and the laurel, as she walked through the woods, she loved them. She did not want to miss the opportunity to notice the first wildflowers, the berries as they ripened, or the small maps the scurrying voles and mice carved in the snow. And she'd come to depend on the wild turkeys that announced themselves outside her window and gathered under the apple tree.

"No," she said, and kissed him. "I have a girlfriend," she lied.

This was not what she had planned to say. But it was true that the companionship she had with Theo was all she wanted at the moment.

He stepped away from her.

"You're a dyke," he said, looking more confused than angry.

"Am I?" She brushed the sweat off her forehead with the back of her hand.

He watched her for a moment, and then walked toward another girl. Hazel danced alone again, but with less intensity this time. The music seemed to be falling from her body, which was now both tense and tired. How had she—or any of the people in this room—earned this freedom of movement, to inhabit one's body and life foremost for one's own purposes?

The slaughterhouse videos and various conversations with Theo played themselves in her mind, an odd juxtaposition. The films elaborated a bit of family history; her grandfather was a forerunner of the faceless men she'd watched. The men had changed and died, but the conveyor belt had never stopped.

Barns are better empty. He said this each time she asked, as a very young child, to have animals in the barn like their neighbors did. Why, she asked. He said nothing and then finally told her what she did not yet know. Animals live in barns until they are killed. The K-word ran through her five-year-old body, a bitter taste she was unprepared for. He was telling her something she was not supposed to know—a grown-up secret. She could feel her mouth twist slightly and her eyes begin to burn. She believed her father was angry with her. By asking, insisting on animals to fill the barn, she had forced him to say a horrible lie.

The animals entered her imagination by degrees, slipping in deeper as she grew. After her father told her the full story of how Liam lost his hand, the story she'd come to think of as Gabriel's good-bye story, she went to her neighbor. He was a friend with a small farm. I want to watch, she said. No, he said and then, because they were friends and she insisted, he said, Yes.

He chose one of the three Herefords. She's ripe, he said. It was done in a back shed. Hazel wore large rubber boots to protect her shoes. She did not close her eyes, but kept them on the large brown eyes of the cow. She believed it would not happen if she kept her eyes open and looked into her brown eyes. Her friend would not be able to do it. But he did. Everyone should see this. I will tell everyone, she thought but didn't, then; she just took the fact in deeper until it lay, an insomniac, next to her seemingly unperturbed form. What could she have done to prevent it? Think of my three young children, he had said, looking her in the eye. They are like baby birds.

She stared at the bottles again. Ruby, emerald, lapis, onyx; glass the colors of magic potions and candy. She remembered her schooling, how she'd been taught nouns were blue and verbs red, or maybe it was the other way around, by teachers who believed she should be taught language in a way that reflected its inner beauty and relation to the child's soul.

The blue cow. The red line of the knife. They'd lied about beauty. And language, language was the greatest liar of all.

6

"I've come to turn myself in," he said, laughing quietly as she opened the door.

When he called, Theo did not make the connection. What a nice voice, was her only thought. But when he showed up at her office on the third floor of the social sciences building, she knew. She could see Hazel in him immediately, not in any specific feature so much as in his general demeanor and his laugh, which was Hazel's laugh. Good-looking, certainly, but in the way of a man on the edge of some nonspecific ruin.

She had tried, for the sake of her friend, to diagnose Gabriel. How conscious were his wanderings? Did he enter fugue states, in which he left not only his physical context but the memory of his identity as well? Theo liked this idea. Hazel shrugged, ever protective of her father. But she enjoyed the musical association of the word, the intricate patterns that made up a loved one, just about any living thing. He sent postcards and went away repeatedly, for long periods of time, Theo pointed out. This was not at all typical. It didn't hold together. Why should it? Hazel said.

His greeting set Theo off balance. Did he know Hazel was looking for him and that she and Hazel were friends? Or was he responding to her latest ad, which now requested, specifically, interviews with meatpackers?

Before going for the interview, which he thought of as a confession, Gabriel went to a chain restaurant to sit and think. He sat at a booth in the back of the drearily lit place, fingering a saltshaker with his fine, almost delicate hands. He had combed his thick, curly black hair back after washing it in a long shower. He was a strikingly handsome man, youthful at fifty-five. He smiled when the waitress flirted with him.

"Just water for now," he said.

"Meeting someone?" The waitress was a woman probably ten years younger, but she looked his age.

Gabriel smiled and gave her a flash of indigo eyes.

He was barely aware of her, though it would be false to say he was unaware of his own attractiveness. He deferred to it, as to a tiresome but useful protector.

Even when he was living in a comfortable farmhouse with his wife and child, Gabriel thought of himself as a hobo, as someone with nothing on the move. Running away at fifteen had left a mark, and he didn't care to tease apart whether it was because of laziness or trauma that it did not fade.

At age fifty he had found himself in a place where he knew no one, except a woman for whom he'd experienced an unrequited love almost three decades earlier. Martha was his first love. She had been kind, willing, but ultimately indifferent in the way of an eighteen-year-old girl full with her own future. Now, at forty-seven and divorced, she was ready. When she heard the unmistakable voice surprise her over the phone and then saw Gabriel on her doorstep waiting to take her out to dinner, she took him in. Gabriel remained merely nostalgic. Martha offered him her second house to live in for less than half the usual rent. He did not ask what her hopes were.

He remembered reclining next to the oval window just over the wing.

"Chicken or beef?" a voice had half-roused him.

He had slept himself into his boyhood bed, a mattress on the floor of the small parlor next to a fire that always seemed to be dying, his father's whiskey breath on his cheek shouting the words, "Wake up boy!"

Through the window, rectangles of land pretended to be still. The geography was abstracted, resembling the home he had never seen. That's what you got from such distance, the illusion of stillness. But everything was moving, everything. He was no different. His father could work magic on the pennywhistle. Play for the solitary bird, play for the stump of their lives left over on the other side, he had instructed Gabriel. Now the whistle was tucked into the pouch in front of him, next to the vomit bag. Leaving was like that.

Gabriel had arrived in Northern California just at the end of El Niño's raging and a couple of months before his fiftieth birthday. He was seeking warmth, the education and anonymity of the city. For two months wind and rain had torn through much of the state. Chunks of coastline had been eaten by the sea. The receding tide exposed a graveyard of seals, seabirds, and other creatures. He saw the damage but had not seen it happen. By the time he arrived the wreckage lay in incongruous sunshine, surrounded by the lush bloom of whatever had benefited from all the rain.

He did not use the words *broken family* or *failed marriage*, and certainly not *desertion*. His need to go away was like the invisible shifting of water and earth that may, or may not, be preparing for disaster. He remembered his wife's hands, the way her fingers looked ugly to him for the first time as she clutched a bucket of stones to her chest that summer afternoon before he left. Her large, forceful hands were what he had first noticed about her, and the change in them— well, he could not look at it squarely.

He had met Petra in a garden in New York, just an hour south of where they would, a year later, purchase an old farmhouse and begin their married life together. He assumed she was a tenant in the large, rambling house, which was owned by a man who lived most of the year in New York City. She was sitting under an old pear tree, the only remaining member of an orchard that had been leveled decades before. She looked up from her book now and again while he worked, her eyes wandering over azaleas, impatiens, lilacs, irises, and a large herb garden. She did not seem to notice him at all, and this pleased him. It set him at ease.

Each day for two weeks he returned at the same time in the late morning to do his work. And every morning she was there, reading, looking up occasionally. Already then Petra adhered strictly to a schedule of working in her studio (which at that time was a corner of the large room she rented) in the morning from six to ten and again in the late afternoon from four to seven. At the time she was between jobs and so had the rest of the day free. To him she was a mysterious woman in a summer dress reading her mornings away, a woman with long, thick brown hair pulled back in a braid, high cheekbones and a broad, Slavic-looking face. He had not fallen in love with a woman since Martha and knew upon seeing Petra that he wanted, as he would tell her later, to journey with her.

"I have finished the work in your garden," he said.

"Well," she said and put down her book.

He invited her to the nearest small town for coffee.

"No, let's stay here," she said. And she showed him the kitchen.

Within a year they were married. Five months later Petra was pregnant with Hazel.

Gabriel was delighted, yet, as the birth grew nearer, a familiar but unrecognizable fear moved him.

I will be back before the baby is born. I am sorry. I love you. G. It had cost him some effort to write these lines free of error. Always, in the back of his mind, he feared Petra laughing at him.

He drove aimlessly into Pennsylvania, Virginia, West Virginia, and back again, sketching plants, documenting the months from late winter to early August when his child was due to be born. The drawings would make a book for mother and baby.

It was not entirely deliberate on his part, staying away just long enough to miss the birth. There had been some getting lost and the striking up of random acquaintances. And the heaviness—something palpable, making it difficult, as in a dream, to move forward.

But he would not speak about any of this to the interviewer. He had come to tell the story of the slunk calf, a story he had not yet repeated to anyone. He came close to telling his daughter the summer she turned fifteen but found he could not. If he'd had whatever it took—courage or will or openness—to tell her or even his wife that summer, when for some reason it had all weighed so heavily on him again, perhaps then he would not have had to go. A reverie of days fell on him, like autumn leaves, like hail; and he sat, unsheltered for a moment, under these days of family life never to be. He hadn't known the phrase "slunk calf" then, when it happened, when he was fifteen; and when he first came across the words in a book had made of them something like "lucks face." When he got it right he looked it up in the dictionary and deciphered the entry. *Slink: to give premature birth to.* Well, that's a lie, he had said out loud to the page. That's a lie.

He ordered a cup of tea.

"Hard decision," the waitress chided.

"Yes, yes," he agreed. "You can't hurry tea." She was not a bad-looking woman. He liked the fact that she had not tried to cover the gray hairs and that she could wear the silly uniform of the place with some dignity. Perhaps she had children to support. Not everyone was as lucky as Petra, making money at something she loved. What did this woman love? He could ask her out rather than go to the interview. But he lost the thought before it had fully formed.

A red candle with white plastic netting stood in the middle of the table, evoking vague yet visceral memories of going to church when he was a small child. He and his mother stopped going for a reason he could not remember. (He never remembered his father going.) Therefore most of what he knew about Catholicism he acquired before the age of six. The religion to him was smells, of incense, candles, and other people's sweat; it was a feeling in his stomach of hunger and another feeling that moved between his gut and his head, often lodging itself right in the throat, a feeling part fear, part excitement when imagining himself in line to open his mouth for the priest. It was the rhythm of words he could not understand spoken by the deep voice. Once he heard the voice speak his own name—Gabriel—and he said, "that's me" too loud. Before he could close his mouth he felt his mother's hand cupping it. "No, not you," she whispered and smiled at him. But he'd heard his name.

Gabriel sat across from Theo in the small room, holding a paper cup of water. She could hear other graduate students chatting in the hallway.

"I'm going to ask you some questions. You only need to answer the ones you can and want to." She spoke her lines, awkwardly.

"No," Gabriel said and looked at her. "I came to tell you a story. If it fits into your survey, that's grand. If not, well, take it home with you anyway."

He called her research a survey, but never mind. It was apt at this point.

Gabriel cleared his throat and took a sip of water.

"I did it to end the shouting between my parents," he began. "They were poor, you see, and my father had recently lost his hand because of a cow who did not want to lose her life. He didn't take to being a cripple gracefully. He drank and there was no money coming in.

"So I went, like he wanted me to, despite my mother's protests, to replace him on the kill floor. I was fifteen. 'No, don't go,' she said. But I got up quietly the next morning and hitched a ride.

"I was given the job of shoveling guts and other waste into a trap in the floor. The foreman handed me a huge shovel and a broom. I couldn't breathe for the smell. I stood among cows hanging upside down bleeding to death. There were those who had not been stunned properly and were being skinned alive. I stood among them. Up to my ankles in blood. I vomited several times. 'You're the man of the house now,' my father had said to me, shaking his stump.

"I pushed my shovel hard as I could and tried not to look at anything. I pushed like a blind man slogging through mud. I did this for a long time. Then I felt something unusually hard stop the shovel." Gabriel's head was bending toward the floor. He spoke as though it had all happened yesterday.

"I opened my eyes. I was pushing a fetal calf, newly ripped from its butchered mother. The calf must have been at term, or very near. When the legs twitched and I saw the head move away from the waste for air, I heard a scream. It seemed to be coming from very far away. The foreman walked over and said, 'What's the matter with you? Keep moving.' And then, again, when I did not move, he said, 'You heard me. Let me see you push it into the trap.' I felt the foreman grab the shovel. He gave one angry push and the calf, covered in blood, disappeared, forefeet first, then the head, resting on the knees.

"That was its life. It was brown and white. Lovely."

Gabriel sat with his elbows on his knees, his hands clasped together. His voice seemed to have a permanent tremble, as though speaking itself were an act of great risk.

Theo was silent for a minute. "And how long did you work there after that?"

"I didn't last the day."

"You mean you never went back?"

"Once a shoveler of guts, always a shoveler of guts, I say. But I'm a gardener. Anyway," he laughed, "it's a shorter story than I thought."

Gabriel seemed to have finished, but Theo watched him, waiting for him to say more.

"I never was a good Catholic. But this was a sin. I was not strong enough to stand up to the foreman. Which is to say to the machine, the whole bloody operation."

Of course not, Theo wanted to say. How could he possibly, especially after all these years, believe that there was anything he could have done?

"The calf didn't have a chance," she said instead. She refrained from beginning the sentence with "obviously."

Why did he come? She had not advertised for men haunted. But this must have come through. Her committee had suggested she interview workers who'd held their jobs for a similar amount of time, but the ad didn't make this clear. This latest ad remained vague, she knew, by her committee's standards, though at least she had narrowed it to meatpackers, to what they referred to as a specific population. Gabriel would skew her sample, and yet he was the perfect subject. He was describing one of those moments that marked the ravishment of a child. This was what she wanted—to know this, to hold it like a specimen, to understand it so that she could use it, somehow, anyhow. She was not going to send him away.

"No, it didn't," he said. "But tell me what gave it the strength to move, to raise its head. And besides, that's a hard one to think about. Not having a chance."

Theo understood now that Gabriel had no idea about her connection to Hazel. He had come to her on his own, separately, in response to her ad, which meant that the meeting would have to remain confidential.

"And so then you left and didn't return?" She wanted more of his story, didn't want him to go.

"Yes. They must've dragged me out. I suppose I fainted, hit my head. I woke up in the parking lot. I couldn't go home so I just kept walking, out of town."

"Why couldn't you go home?"

"Hell."

He rose to go.

She handed him a check and invited him to call if he wanted to say more or ask questions.

"It's a shorter story than I imagined it to be," he said again. He handed her the check back.

She did not want him to go, she felt again. Her reasons were confused. No one over forty-five should be that good looking, especially not Hazel's father. He was so handsome she believed he might cure her nausea and exhaustion. Same old stupid religion, she told herself. Still, if not for her attraction, she was sure she would have wept. And then, maybe partly because of it, she did tear up, knowing it was not about the cow and calf, both of whom she was trying hard not to picture.

"What a story." She found herself wanting to tell him she was pregnant, and then heard herself telling him, as an explanation for her tears, and as a way of breaking out of the grim, oppressive subject, "I'm pregnant—a little emotional lately."

"Very nice for you," he said, one hand on the door. He wore the beginnings of a smile, out of confusion, it seemed to Theo, more than anything else.

*

"Dance me a jig," Gabriel would say to Hazel sometimes when either of them was glum. Her father would begin lifting one knee and then a foot into the air, coming down on the wooden floor with a sure, light tap. She would join in. Sometimes they'd take out their whistles and play while they danced. If Petra was around she'd stand by and watch, clapping her hands.

Hazel was in the park, sitting on a bench. A woman stood between her and the remaining cows with her two small children. The animals milled about, everyone moving more slowly in the heat. She was glad to see Patch had not been replaced yet.

If we forget about you, about what really happens to you, she said silently to the animals at large, *we forget our own hearts. It should be obvious that this is immediate or eventual suicide.*

She was restless. She had a simple idea. Next time she visited the park she would wear a sign. The sign would have a picture of a juicy steak or hamburger with an arrow pointing toward the live cows. "Make the Connection," her sign would say.

Back at the house, a woman was clipping hedges, her hair spilling toward the grass. Hazel cleared her throat but said nothing.

"Hi." The woman straightened when she saw Hazel. "Can I help you with something?"

Hazel did not move from the curb. "No. Just admiring your garden." She walked on. Hazel had begun to grow accustomed to her father's unconfirmed absence, and she did not want to acknowledge the various possibilities this woman signified.

An hour later, when she returned, the woman was gone. Hazel went back to the deck. The papers she had stacked were still there. She wondered whether the woman had noticed them. She sat down and lifted the top paper onto her lap. It was refolded loosely and incorrectly. She began shuffling through the others to see if they, too, had been read.

When someone you love disappears, you look anywhere for clues. Martha watched Hazel through the window. The strange girl was trespassing, but Martha's first thought was not a thought at all, but a feeling of embarrassment. She was remembering how she had gone through the papers, looking for she knew not what. For his obituary, maybe. Woman reads of long ago lover's death in the newspaper. The man had recently come back into her life, the story would continue. He was renting a house from her. She was his landlady and link to something he refused to let go of. And then he disappeared from the house. Gabriel O'Connell, found dead in a bungalow in southern Mexico. She could picture the font used to bring the news. Had he even been to Mexico? He sent her a card from there once, so surely he had. But she didn't really know where he traveled.

"What are you doing here?"

Hazel recognized the woman's voice. She was standing by the open French window.

Hazel did not know how to answer her question.

Martha stepped out of the window and onto the deck.

She was this girl's age when Gabriel had loved her. She had never been as striking as this girl, more ordinarily pretty, as she was now ordinarily middle-aged.

"Is this your house?" Hazel ventured. "I thought it was empty."

"Yes, yes it is. I rent it out. My tenant is away."

Hazel knew then.

"Come in and have something to drink." Martha felt drawn to the girl.

Hazel did not recognize anything in the large living room as belonging to her father.

Martha went to the adjacent kitchen. "At least he doesn't leave food to rot," she said, comparing to her ex-husband. She poured Hazel a glass of ice water. "He likes to live mostly in one room, it seems," she added, needing to speak of him.

Hazel sipped the water. She could see through the door into a small bedroom. His plaid shirt was draped over a chair, and several pairs of shoes were lined up neatly. He always chose his shoes carefully and took good care of them. Hazel remembered that shirt. He'd worn it so often she could see, even from where she was sitting, the chair back through it. It was green and gray and almost as thin as gossamer, almost that beautiful.

"So tell me, what are you doing here?" Martha was still thinking of Gabriel. She looked at the girl and felt embarrassed once more because she knew she wanted more than anything at that moment to be that girl's age again.

"Animal advocacy work." Hazel could erase him like that, with a true sentence. Not as punishment, but to set them both free. "I mean I'm hoping to—find some."

"*I* mean what were you doing on my deck."

"I've moved from the East Coast and am looking for work. I shouldn't have been reading through your papers. I'm sorry. When I could have gone to any coffee shop and read the want ads."

Martha looked at Hazel and felt, oddly, that she'd seen her before.

Hazel did not identify herself or ask about the absent tenant.

7

"Oh my." The doctor spoke not to her but to the technician.

"Just tell me what's wrong," Theo whispered. She was lying on the examination table. It frightened her, the way her belly still flattened in this position.

"Everything is all right." These were his first kind words. She was overly grateful for them.

"Listen," he said.

The heartbeat sounded incredibly fast and irregular.

"What's wrong with the baby's heart?"

"Nothing. There are two hearts. You're carrying twins. We'll do an ultrasound next time.

"You can get dressed now."

The doctor left the room.

Dressed, she sat in his office.

"Remember we consider twins a high-risk pregnancy. It's doubly," he smiled, "important that you eat well, get plenty of rest, and do not smoke or drink. There is a chance we'll have to put you on bed rest in the later months." She drank in these, to her, motherly words.

Planning to quit, she had lied to him about smoking. At the moment she was craving a cigarette very badly. One more to get me over the news and then that's it, she thought.

Outside, she could smoke only half. She'd never been a heavy smoker. She walked to a nearby playground and threw the pack into a trashcan. She chose a bench near a few children climbing on a wooden jungle gym. A little further away, two mothers pushed their babies in swings. Soon this would be her world. But two! She didn't know how it could be done. One hand on one rump, the other on another, pushing the swings toward the sky, while her heart spread like the wings of a bird. Where was M now, the breeder? What did it matter? He had stayed long enough to convince her he was capable of being a good man.

She wanted to tell someone her news, someone other than young Hazel. The friends she'd made were mostly other graduate students, or friends from her undergraduate days, but they were not close friends. Telling them would not be that satisfying. It occurred to her that it took Hazel moving in with her to create even the semblance of a close friendship. Theo had a reputation, because no one knew her very well, of being a very serious, hard-working, and somewhat aloof student.

She wanted to tell her. *Mom, I am*—but, even if she could, her mother would have said something cutting, reflecting, as always, disappointment with Theo.

With the first shock of her mother's death, she remembered now, there had also come a thrill, as though something had happened at last that came close to matching Theo's inner life. There was an initial desire to call the news; and then, after some time passed, she found she did not want to and could not tell anyone.

Her mother had one friend, a neighbor whose children would play with her children, and who would bring her novels and an occasional martini. "C'mon, you got to live a little," Theo heard her say once as she handed her mother a drink. She knew how to enjoy herself, this woman did. Virginia was large and spacious like the western state she had come from, and she made the eastern suburb stretch to fit.

Back and forth, she watched the babies swing. The mothers talked to one another.

Theo used to like to hang upside down and look at the world that way. There was a playground near the American army base in the German town where her grandmother lived. She would hang from the monkey bars and look for the windows of her grandmother's apartment, which was across the road. The rectangular balconies at the front of each unit, and the entire postwar structure, looked more or less the same whether she was upside down or not. Only the location of ground and sky told her for sure from which angle she was looking. It was a game she played with herself, to find her grandmother's particular balcony, the one from which her grandmother waved to them each time they arrived and departed, *die Enkelkinder aus Amerika*, the grandchildren from America. When she swung down to land, the backs of her knees were often raw. It was a feeling she savored because it contained confident anticipation of this small pain getting better. Her skin would sting in the bathtub and then, under her grandmother's cool sheets, there would be only a slight and fading discomfort.

A woman was bent over her small boy. His plump legs dangled from the stroller parked near Theo's bench. The boy wore a sun hat like the one her brother wore at about that age. Oma had given it to Martin the summer she first met him, and he wore it the morning their mother took her three children to the cemetery. Oma, to Theo's disappointment, stayed behind. Their father had gone to meet an old army buddy for an afternoon beer. He had no interest in visiting what he referred to as the other side's dead.

Theo remembered looking down at the blue and yellow stripes of Martin's hat when they came to a stop in front of the gravestones. The hat had been waiting, wrapped in blue paper, when they arrived a week earlier. Theo received a red purse, which she carried with her that afternoon, and Johanna an identical green one, which she unwrapped and immediately put aside. Martin's hat had a narrow rim to guard from sun and a tie to help it stay on. It framed his strawberry blond hair and round face nicely. Every now and then their mother adjusted it, although it did not need adjusting.

Identical flat stones marked the graves of Theo's uncles. They were eighteen and nineteen years old when they were killed at the Russian Front. Theo's grandfather's larger stone stood to the right. Martin sat in his stroller, his head growing heavy. Johanna skipped down the gravel path, kicking some of the stones into the air as she went along. Theo waited, almost hoped, for their mother to snap at Johanna, but she did not. It was Theo she focused on, the quiet older daughter who stood obediently gazing at the three stones. Theo could feel something coming, as she almost always could, a sensation of heat crawling up the back of her neck.

"Are you just going to stand there?" It was said in the tone that told Theo anything was possible.

Not knowing what her mother wants, Theo does not answer. She stiffens, freezes like any trapped animal. She is eight years old. Her mother, holding a bouquet of daffodils in one hand, daisies in the other, wears a matching yellow dress and sun hat. She is beautiful; how can Theo be so afraid? The thought blows under her eyelids and is blinked away. Her mother pushes the daisies into her hand, causing Theo to drop the red purse.

"Take these. Don't just stand there! Pay your respects." Stand. There. The words enter and make her weak. It is not all right to be there, as she is, just standing.

She gives Theo what must have been only a light push forward, but Theo stumbles and is on her knees in the middle of the brothers' shared plot. Before she can stand, her mother is grabbing her shoulder. At first she seems to be pulling Theo up, but then she begins pushing her down further into the grass. She pushes Theo down until Theo's face is watering grass and dirt. Theo can no longer see the flowers she is crushing in her hand, trapped between ribs and ground. Her mother holds on until the top of Theo's head lightly grazes one of the stones. She gives one last push, actually hitting Theo's head against the stone this time, and then she lets Theo go. Her head does not hit hard, but she wonders whether she is bleeding. And the world goes dark. Then her mother is tugging at her yellow dress, wiping her face with a handkerchief. She is moaning, *Ach, du hast keine Ahnung.* You have no idea.

Martin, wailing in his stroller.

"Get up," she says to Theo, "people are coming."

Once she sees Theo can stand, she takes Martin out of his stroller and coos at him. Then, as though nothing happened, or as though inflicting what she did on Theo somehow set her right again inside, she shouts cheerily, "Jo-han-na," letting the second syllable crescendo and rise in pitch.

"Johanna, put these flowers on your uncle's graves. Show your sister how it is done."

Johanna unselfconsciously picks up the daisies, which Theo left strewn on the grass mound, and plops them between the two stones.

"Let's play," Johanna says to Theo. She takes Theo by the hand and they run, as if together, as if they didn't have two different mothers.

Later that day her mother takes her aside and says, as Theo stiffens, "You were my first baby. You know how much I love you."

Theo watched the woman pick up her boy and carry him to the sandbox. The woman placed a blue pail and shovel in front of the child, kneeling down beside him and running sand through her fingers with what seemed to Theo great tenderness. It was late afternoon now, getting cooler. Theo put her palms over her bloated abdomen and felt her breath moving it up and down. Careless woman, what had she done?

*

Hazel absentmindedly took Johanna's cards out of the shoebox that still lay on the coffee table. It calmed her to arrange them neatly, in rows. When she finished she walked into the kitchen. Theo was doing dishes.

"He *is* living there," Hazel said.

Theo flushed. She would not tell Hazel about Gabriel coming for an interview. At least not yet. The rules of confidentiality forbade it, conveniently for her.

Hazel sat in the cushioned wooden chair she'd found free on the curb a few days earlier.

"So you finally saw him?" Theo asked.

"No. His landlady let me in. His things are still there. Even his whistle." Hazel had taken a closer look at the room while Martha was in the bathroom.

Theo clanked a few dishes in the sink.

A day did not go by without Hazel picking up her instrument. The same was true, she said, of her father.

"It seems to me a man who is capable of leaving his daughter would have no difficulty trashing a piece of tin. I'm sorry. He may be good-looking, but he's an idiot."

"How do you know he's good-looking?"

"I just assume, with a daughter like you . . . "

They were silent for a while, Theo convinced she'd blown it. But, lucky for her, Hazel had a very unsuspecting mind.

"Did I ever tell you my brother is a violinist? I mean, speaking of instruments. He has a gig with a major orchestra in a city I've never been to. Sometimes he sends me a postcard when he's on tour."

Not long after their mother died, their father came home with a long, rectangular gift for Martin. Nothing for Theo, but she loved her brother so much she almost didn't care. He always preferred her lap, throwing his arms around her neck and saying earnestly, I love you Ona. He opened his gift and inside was a shiny new half-size violin. The way the instrument rested on its bed of imitation satin reminded Theo of a wake she'd been to for the grandmother of a Catholic friend. Unable to look at the dead woman, she stared at the glossy material surrounding her instead.

When her brother saw the instrument he looked at Theo as if to say, now what? "Take it to school, son, and get yourself some lessons," their father said. Their mother used to play her classical records often. The sounds of the German, French and Russian composers wove through the rooms of the house, but it was Martin who, already at age two and a half, sat with his ear to the speaker and listened.

The next morning Martin got onto the school bus, his knapsack covering his small, thin back and his violin case hanging from his right hand. She could tell he liked carrying it. Theo kissed him on the back of the head before the bus doors closed on the grade school children. The violin would take him from her. The small boy turned into a serious musician almost overnight. When she drew him onto her lap he acquiesced but was elsewhere, she could tell, and not only because he was getting older. He could sense her jealousy and envy, the way she coveted the old affection as well as his new passion. He withdrew. By the time she understood this, it was too late. When he wrote, he addressed her with his old baby name for her, Ona. It was the only rag left from their childhood affinity.

"How come you never learned to play an instrument?" Hazel asked.

Theo shrugged. She regretted mentioning Martin. It only depressed her.

"So did you find out where he is?" Theo tried to sound casual.

"No."

"I'm sure you'll meet up with him any day now. He's obviously around."

"No, he's obviously not around. Otherwise I would have seen him."

"Well, did you ask his landlady where he is?"

"She doesn't know." Hazel was quiet for a moment and then said, "He's cheated on my Mom. I hate him for that."

"You must have known, given that he's been away for five years, that this was a possibility."

From Hazel's silence, it was clear to Theo that Hazel had, in fact, not considered this, whether out of willful blindness or complete naiveté, she did not know.

"Why don't we go together," Hazel suggested. "I mean you and Job and your baby and me."

"Go where?"

"Back East. You could have your baby in your home state. My mother has a friend who's a wonderful midwife. We could be a little family, for a little while anyway."

Theo stopped doing dishes but did not turn around.

"Babies," she corrected Hazel. "I've got two in here."

"Oh my goodness." Hazel walked up to Theo and hugged her from behind. She could feel Theo startle.

"Double joy," Hazel said. "I'll make some tea. You sit down."

"Don't act like I'm sick," Theo said. "I get enough of that from the doctor."

"Well, the midwife . . . " Hazel began.

"Hazel," Theo interrupted.

"Wouldn't treat you like that," Hazel finished. "Just say you'll think about it."

"OK, I'll think about it," Theo said and let the rest go.

The cards laid out on the coffee table reminded Theo of her own arrangement years earlier. When she saw the thin red line and when she heard the word *twins*, her first thoughts were Johanna, Martin. The fact of her pregnancy would resurrect her family; they would gather around her. It did not take long for her to dismiss the fantasy. But she had gone to the cards once again to find her sister there and to contemplate sending her the news.

"Getting ready for solitaire?" Theo was irritated. The cards were off-limits.

"When are you going to go see her?" Hazel asked, ignoring Theo's irritation.

"Not anytime soon," Theo replied and looked down at her belly. "The doctor thinks I'll be lying in bed all day before too long."

Hazel rolled her eyes. "Does your sister have children?"

"I don't know."

"You don't know?"

"I thought of visiting her years ago, but—I was ill." As she said this, Theo realized the truth of it.

"What was the matter with you?"

"Everything."

"Surely your sister would have written if she'd had children."

"Why would you, of all people, say that? Human beings are capable of severing the deepest connections, at least physically. It's a peculiar way we have of denying there is an inside, a landscape drawn in great detail from the past."

"Or of asserting our freedom," Hazel countered.

Theo scooped the cards back into the box, counting. Except for the one of her mother's village, which hung on the wall, they were all there.

8

He knew this moment would come—though he did not imagine it would occur while he performed, without thinking, the most everyday of gestures.

Gabriel was in front of the house tying his sneaker. Since coming to California he had taken up running, sometimes with Martha, who was an avid jogger. Today he would run alone, with the image of the young, dark-haired woman who interviewed him still close. He stood up and saw her.

Hazel had just come from the park, where she was laughed at and then asked by a park official to leave. She still carried the sign, but upside down now.

"Hello, little faerie."

If Hazel were able to find her voice, it would be the voice of someone addressing a stranger.

She had to look down at him slightly, having grown two inches taller than he.

"You've grown . . . Or maybe I'm shrinking. Practically an old man now." He laughed. His eyes looking at her were sad.

"You look good," she said finally.

"Tart little liars, sometimes, the looks," he said. "Would you like to join me for a run?"

He did not seem to notice the sign, which she leaned on now as though it were a walking stick.

"It's been five years." She let that out, at least that.

Gabriel looked uncomfortable, fearing accusation.

"You've come a long way," he said and opened his arms to her.

She hesitated and then stepped toward him, letting him enclose her. His arms were light as paper. They moved apart.

"When I left you were the same age I was when I ran away from home. Fifteen."

"What?" Hazel shook her head, taking the sentence apart to make sense of it. When I left you. When I left, you . . .

"I've often thought about that," he said. "How's the old goat?" He was referring to the one animal that occupied their barn. Gabriel had brought him home from a yard sale not long before he drove off. This one came to me, was the explanation he gave when she questioned him about putting an animal into the barn.

"Fine. We've been taking good care of him."

He stood there, ready for his jog. It would not have occurred to him to change his plan, to invite her in.

"Why did you send the card?"

"It was a dream I had."

The card was a dream. She knew what he meant, that he left out "because of"—that he did not speak of causes, of action and consequence.

"Mom and I are not a dream."

Spanish was still coursing through him, though he understood very little. English seemed almost a stranger. He'd just returned. How could he know what to say, or do? She was a young woman now, though he could still see the small girl, whose coming into the world he'd missed. Whose littleness and innocence he'd prized above all else.

Why don't we go for a run together? But he didn't invite her again; or anyway she didn't answer. He'd heard her voice say "we're not a dream," and it made him tense as though at the beginning of a race. He felt poised to run, despite himself.

OK, why don't we go for a run together? She could have said this and they'd be off, jogging up and down the hills, past the smell of eucalyptus and magnolia, into the green park, not to the little zoo, but into the wild trails that were long enough to hold both their stories, the five years, the twenty years, long enough for them to get lost in together and come out again, together, father and daughter. But she had the awkward sign, the wrong sneakers, and jeans that were too tight for running.

"Well, then, we're both here now. I will see you."

And he was off, as though he'd never extended her an invitation, however slight.

Hazel stood leaning on her sign and watched his receding figure. It was a relief to admit he was no longer worth her trouble.

*

After his jog, Gabriel walked to *The Owl*. The restaurant/bar was a fiesta in itself, and Gabriel had been a regular ever since discovering it by chance not long after arriving in California. It filled with everyone and anyone. Always colorful, it was sometimes a safe harbor, other times ready to erupt with unarticulated despair or any species of friction. Gabriel stood among a small group of migrant workers from Mexico, almost old friends now. The men picked strawberries and artichokes. One of the men explained that he had found more permanent work as a meatpacker.

Gabriel had first met these men several months before, and they told him about their lives and their jobs using hand signals and pen on bar napkins. "Go there," one of the men said when Gabriel asked about Mexico. "See for yourself. It is beautiful." He drew a map of Mexico and the location of his village on the back of a coaster. Motion and luck, they tasted good to a man, almost like hope.

By the third drink, he could no longer be sure he'd seen his daughter. Had it really been her, or rather his erratic and sudden absorption in his image of her, which took hold repeatedly but unpredictably? Where had he been when Hazel was searching for him? He hardly knew himself. If he thought about it, and if he was told he had not been at Martha's, he could bring into awareness the fact that he'd driven south. He'd stopped in coastal towns, watched a man making a sand sculpture, and walked the beaches. He slept in his car. He crossed the border and, after days of haphazard travel, found the bungalow to which he'd been directed by one of the men at *The Owl*. While there, he had a dream about his wife and daughter. After a night with the singing woman, he dreamed his wife was pregnant again.

He stayed in a small bungalow outside a village not far from the sea.

He set out early each day. Sometimes he rode an old bicycle that had been left leaning against the wall, but mostly he walked. He walked up the hill past other thatched bungalows and people sitting or working outside, past chickens who sometimes followed him up the dirt road a bit, and past the neighbor's donkey. Once on the other side of the hill, he found himself by the sea edged with a long line of palms. When he was hungry he stopped for a picnic of fruit and bread, sometimes cheese and even sausage. He followed his lunch with a siesta, drifting off to sleep in the warm shade, not lost, yet not knowing exactly where he was either. He returned to the bungalow each evening just as it was getting dark and sat outside for another hour or two watching the stars emerge.

The bungalow had one room that was kitchen, dining room, and bedroom. There was an outhouse about ten paces from the only door. Opposite his bed, resting incongruously on two large crates, was a television. After supper he often turned it on, lying back on his bed, switching channels periodically. Often he fell asleep like this, to the comforting sound of Spanish voices. Sometimes, when he felt safe enough, he clicked it off soon after clicking it on and lay in the dark listening for whatever came to break the stillness. He heard the mysterious communications of animals he couldn't identify and, once, distant singing. He'd gone out that night to get closer to the singing, and found himself in a small neighborhood of bungalows at the center of which a group of women sang in a loose circle, while a single drummer kept rhythm. From the group the most beautiful and perhaps the youngest followed him back to his bungalow. The touch of youth, touching it all over, had made him sob after she'd gone. The woman whose name he did not ask returned several times, comforting him, exhausting him.

His neighbor with the donkey was about the age Gabriel's father would have been if he were still alive. The donkey, too, was old. Gabriel imagined it had been a long friendship between the man and the donkey, sure as the smell of wet dust after one of the fierce, quick rains. They lived on top of the small hill and just up the road from Gabriel's door. Gabriel could see, nightly, the man's hands resting on the donkey's back, their small figures turning to silhouettes as he waited for the stars.

It was a strange feeling, to call hello to a man who could be his father and to have no father left. But of course it was so. He was fifty-five years old. Liam had been dead for over a decade, his mother not so long. He was in the front line now, and how could it be? Even plant time cycled through too fast: seed, sprout, flower, fruit; spring into summer into fall. In New England the end of summer felt like falling off high scaffolding surrounding a house that would never get built, like in that poem Petra had copied out for him before they married. And fall, in all its glory, you watched it as you yourself were falling, awaiting the cold, hard stillness—not without its relief—of winter.

Once the man walked toward his bungalow and called him over. They had both stood watching the sun go down, Gabriel at the foot of the rise and the man at the top. The man said something Gabriel did not understand and pointed to the donkey who, as Gabriel got closer, he could see looked thin and worn, hip bones and rib cage bulging out. The man pointed to the animal's eyes and Gabriel could see that they were running, not with a clear liquid but with some kind of puss that also coated part of the eyeball. Gabriel wasn't sure whether the man was asking for help or whether he just wanted company, someone to appreciate his friend, who was possibly dying. The man began leading the donkey, and it walked slowly and with difficulty, toward a small barn.

It was almost dark in the barn, with just enough light coming through so they could move around without stumbling. The fresh hay smell reminded Gabriel of walking past long stretches of farmland when he had first hitchhiked out of Chicago. He had slept among its sweet smell those summer nights and then in the brisk fall, struggling to stay warm.

When they reached the corner where the straw bedding was spread, the man took down a large wool blanket that was hanging from a peg and laid it on the donkey's back. All along the man was muttering softly to himself, repeating a word Gabriel could barely make out, something like Alma, in a tone that led him to assume this was the animal's name. Later he would learn that Alma had been the name of the man's wife, who had died two years earlier.

The donkey lay down as soon as the blanket was on her. The man kneeled and gestured for Gabriel to do the same. He hesitated, but acquiesced. The man pressed his hands firmly together, and Gabriel could see they were trembling. He touched his old friend's gray, dusty forehead and cupped one hand over each afflicted eye, but did not close them. The man closed his eyes, which were small and surrounded by deep creases. He remained on his knees, silent but for occasional murmuring addressed to the animal, his dead wife, or God—Gabriel didn't know which. After about ten minutes he crossed himself and stood up. Gabriel also stood up and followed the old man out of the barn. His body was still warm and full with the woman. When they were outside, the man pointed down the hill toward Gabriel's bungalow. He was letting Gabriel know it was time for him to go. The old man went back into the barn to wait, alone now, with his friend.

The following day, when Gabriel looked over to where the donkey and the man had stood each evening, there was only the bald hill with the late sun beginning to darken it.

Theo and M had gone to *The Owl* for their fateful beer, and now Theo sat at the bar again, sipping the one drink per week she allowed herself and soaking in the music, deliberately letting it empty her mind of thought. It was indeed like a hot bath, and soon, sufficiently warmed and relaxed, she would turn her thoughts to the father of her children, to her children, to her research—her life in its new emerging shape. Everyone wants to rewrite some version of the Story. That is a lifetime's work. This is just a dissertation. She heard the voice of her Advisor. He was a kind man with a sense of humor, but he'd gotten irritated when she told him she'd begun interviewing people. "About what? You don't have a coherent proposal." When she decided, given the way the cards had fallen, to focus her research on meatpackers, her advisor became suspicious. Why meatpackers? You don't have an ax to grind, do you? I'm retiring soon and don't have time for that. No, she assured him, it just evolved out of circumstance. Not a very scholarly or scientific approach, he'd retorted, but let's see what you do.

The father of my children. Theo rolled the words around in her mind. *The Owl* was the only place she had ever seen M outside of her office and her bedroom. I have two children growing inside me from an almost anonymous seed. That sounded quite dramatic. Then, add this: anonymous but for the knowledge that he was a poor man who, among other things, had slaughtered for a living and saved the life, sort of, of one chicken. She looked around the place, knowing she would need to describe it someday to her children when they demanded to know something about their father, and saw Gabriel standing with a group of men at the other end of the very long bar.

Gabriel was a distraction, and Theo had always been vulnerable to distractions. She was not sure whether to draw attention to herself. She knew that even if she were to catch his eye, he would not move toward her. He was not a man who made advances. He was a man who waited. She watched Gabriel cavorting among the Mexicans, and thought about M. What if he returned?

He placed in front of her a plate containing a large boiled artichoke and pasta with tomato sauce. Gabriel had seen her sitting at the bar, the woman to whom he'd told the story of the slunk calf, and he did not hesitate. He ordered them each a dinner and brought it over to Theo. His companions fell away. Once he made his mind up about a woman, he was like a child absorbed and utterly confident in his play.

"You shouldn't be drinking, in your condition."

Theo startled at the sudden sound of his voice so close and the sight of steaming food.

Her condition. She had to laugh.

"Not even a little? The French recommend a small glass of red wine a day for women in my *condition*."

"That does not look like red wine." He put the plate down in front of her. "Just south of here is artichoke country," he explained, as though the fact she was a student also made her a tourist. "I like to drive down there and buy them by the side of the road. There's a small restaurant that specializes in artichoke dishes when they're in season. Artichoke salad, artichoke pasta, artichoke soup, stuffed artichoke. Artichoke pudding."

"That's nice," Theo said. "Obsessive; I can relate."

"But these are good, too."

She looked at her artichoke as though it were a complicated puzzle she did not have the patience to do. The thing was still steaming, forcing into her nose its strangely non-foodlike smell. Theo had not eaten many artichokes, but she remembered liking them OK.

They began plucking leaves and raking them through their teeth. Theo's stomach turned in unison with her swallowing.

"I'll show you the correct way to eat the heart," Gabriel said.

"I'm never going to get there. Sorry. I can't eat this." She pushed her plate away. "It's pregnancy."

"Never mind," he said. "How about some spaghetti?"

This she could eat, but only the parts not touching the sauce.

"Theo is a scientist," Gabriel was explaining to several of the men who had drifted back toward him. She could not abide it when psychologists referred to themselves as scientists. The entire vague, lumpy signifier seemed suspect to her. She thought of it as a euphemism for trying to get away with something—a huge sum of grant money, for example.

Nonetheless, she decided to play it up, the scientist introduction. Already they were looking at her with a mixture of suspicion and curiosity.

"I am doing some research," she said, "about people . . ." What should she say next?

"I am paying people twenty-five dollars to do a one-hour interview with me," she said instead. Theo could see the scowl on her advisor's face. "To talk about what you do in the world. If any of you are interested, here is my card." She assumed some of them were meatpackers. But she'd done it again, gone vague and inclusive. She was reluctant to specify. She could not quite get herself to say out loud: I am writing a dissertation about meatpackers. How limited. She wanted to write about children.

She'd had the cards made on her committee's recommendation. Remember, one of them had said, you are a professional. She thought immediately of hookers and then of how nicely dressed her therapist always was. Theo had gone for about twenty sessions and never saw her repeat an outfit.

"Twenty-five dollars an hour," a blond man repeated. "Sure, I'll talk to you. Do you know how many cows I have to send to cow heaven to earn that? What do you want to know?"

"Not here," Theo said. "Call me in my office and we can arrange a time."

She sounded so above it all, the scientist with money to spare. She did not say, your colleague is the father of my children.

She'd believed she was in love with M when her children were conceived. This fact pleased her. And it was convenient that she no longer harbored this illusion. She decided her love for M was something like her mother looking for her pulse. The big difference, of course, being that her mother ended up dead and Theo with the beginnings of two new lives. She felt, suddenly, amazingly, undeservedly lucky.

"Let's take a walk," Gabriel said, as though they were alone.

Theo hesitated. "OK, a short walk. I'm very tired and I need to get home."

Theo would never walk the marina alone at night. Walking its paths, looking out over the bay, was one of those things she could only do with a man, or perhaps a tall woman, at her side.

"I would never come here alone at night." She spoke her thought to Gabriel.

"No," he said.

"And this is one of my favorite spots."

"It is lovely, isn't it?"

They walked out on the pier and watched the city across the water obscured by a gathering mist. The damp air enclosed them. She stopped to rest against a railing. He moved next to her and she, despite herself, leaned into him. His arm went around her and she spun to face him. She could see droplets of water on his dark hair.

"Theo," he said, with that slight lisp. And that was it. His lips covered hers, cupping, for an instant, the entire sea.

She allowed herself this and then, doing what she had not thought possible, pushed him away gently. It was an unfamiliar, protective gesture.

"I know your daughter," she said. "Hazel is living with me, looking for you."

He looked at her intently.

She found she was angry at the yearning in his eyes, at his silence. "Why did you abandon your daughter?"

"That's a psychologist's word," he smiled. "I had a dream about you when I was in Mexico. It was about you and my daughter. I thought it was about my wife, but it must have been about you."

Gabriel had seen two figures coming up over the rise past his neighbor's house, like the shadows of two large birds, wingless, but birdlike nonetheless, for they seem to have landed out of the nowhere of the sky. It was not until they came closer that he recognized his daughter. She had never come looking for him before. He was afraid. He could not move toward her. She was with a woman. The woman was pregnant. He remembered thinking he had expected a man and also that the pregnant woman should not be walking here, so far from medical help. The two women held hands, as though to steady each other. We will leave in the morning, his daughter said. We are just passing through. He gave the pregnant woman his bed for the night and slept on the floor. His daughter insisted on sleeping outside. He wanted badly to go out and check on her, the way he had so often checked for her breathing when she was a wee thing. But again he couldn't move. His legs were as if in mud. When he finally did go out at dawn she had already left; all he saw was the reddish earth and patches of long, dry grass flattened by her shape.

He remembered his dream and needed to wake up from it afresh. He looked down at the water behind Theo's legs.

"Don't tell me your dream." She kissed his eyelids. "Anyway, what do you have to say? Your daughter is staying with me because she traveled all this way and didn't find you."

"After that dream I wrote her the card," Gabriel continued, as if he hadn't heard, "that brought her here." He'd crossed the border into California, walked the beaches and bought the card. After mailing it, he found he was not yet ready to return to the address that he'd sent his daughter.

Hazel had shown Theo that card when, after a week had gone by with no sign of her father, Theo accused Hazel of making the whole thing up. She had no father here, but was using the story as an excuse to move in with her. Theo remembered looking at the familiar image of the Golden Gate Bridge rising out of the fog and at Gabriel's cryptic and, she would have to say, cruel message. A father who has disappeared for five years was responsible for saying more than "I am thinking of you."

"I have seen her," Gabriel continued, as though he were still speaking of his dream. "She walked up to the house." He said, "the house," as though Theo should know what he was referring to.

They began walking back toward land and his car. The mist turned to rain.

"No, I don't want a lift, thank you." Saying no to Gabriel felt like filling her lungs to a capacity she did not know they had, and then releasing.

"You know she's going to go home soon. And I might go with her."

Gabriel did not react when she said this. He stood looking into the distance.

"What's the matter with you!" She was suddenly angry. "Call your daughter! How do you think it feels for her to have come all this way . . . " She tried to run, but Gabriel held her arm.

"Careful," he said. "Could be slippery."

It was easy to pull away.

Soon he would drive south again, down the reassuring blandness of the freeway, along the beautiful coastal route, toward heat and the border. Without knowing the language or almost anything about the culture he is drawn there, as he was to California, by anonymity and motion, as though together they could create another dimension—bloodless, timeless, and silent, yet filled with scents of green. The outlines of his daughter and Theo, too sharp, will cut into the back he turns on them. He will begin to mark time's passing by the fetal month; he will imagine vividly, as a landscape already lived in completely, how much her body has swelled, the size of the baby. And he will try, without luck, to imagine the father.

9

Theo sat by the kitchen window in her bathrobe drinking a fake coffee drink. How would the night have passed had she accepted the ride from Gabriel? There would have come a point, she knew this, at which he would disappear. Yet he had brought the plates, something she never would have expected, lovely plates of food she could not eat.

Hazel came through the front door and down the hallway and fell into the chair across from her. She put her head down on the small table. When she looked up, her jaw resting in her palms, Theo could see a scratch running the length of her left cheek.

"What happened to you?"

Hazel sat up straight and looked at her.

"I was at the university, at a vigil for laboratory animals, and then outside the house of a so-called scientist—a fancy house, not far from where my father pretends to be staying."

Theo sighed in exasperation. She could tell Hazel was going to go on again about things she didn't particularly care to hear. She looked at Hazel again and could see that, scratch aside, she looked ravaged and so pale her freckles seemed to be floating.

"Are you OK? Do you want some ice?"

Hazel did not answer.

Was it the strain of the strange journey to find her father that had led to this, to what Theo perceived as a reckless desperation? She had the thought and knew, immediately, how insulting it would be to Hazel, or any activist. Who wanted their passions psychoanalyzed?

Still, she said, "You'll see your father again and talk. I'm sure that's what he wants—what he's waiting for."

"What? Who's thinking about him?"

Hazel had told her how they'd met, finally and uneventfully, in front of that house. He'd been tying his sneaker, getting ready to jog. They'd had a short conversation and gone their separate ways. He had offered no apologies, as far as Theo could tell. It seemed unreal, the way Hazel described it. How could she ever tell Hazel now what happened between them? Aside from kissing her, he'd gone out of his way for her, a stranger—perhaps because she was a stranger.

"Someone distributed photographs of the animals. It was unbelievable. I thought this was a progressive place—the sixties and all that." Hazel fell silent, and Theo tried to picture her standing or sitting outside the building where she'd had several psychology classes. She'd only had one class involving animals—mice—and had had to kill (of course that word was not used) only one. At the time, she found it not so much cruel as terribly tedious, unconnected to anything that interested her even remotely. So she went through the motions—jotting down observations of the creatures' reaction to stress—automatically, feeling and learning nothing.

"I cannot explain what it was like to sit outside that building for twelve hours with nothing but a candle. The animals are inside, and if we choose nonviolence there's no way to free them. They remain inside, and we are outside. It sends me to such a dark place, Theo. The strange thing is, it's a place I'm not sure I want to return from, not without a plan. There I feel closest to the animals, to what they must endure."

"Everyone enters pain—injustice, whatever—through their own door," Theo answered, somewhat glibly. "Look at what people do to each other. Is it any wonder what they do to animals?"

"But many people who marched for peace won't march for the animals' peace.

Anyway, is that supposed to be a comfort? Or a justification?"

"No, just something to think about."

"I understand why some groups resort to violence. I can see how it presents the only alternative to an unlivable place."

"You've got to turn your mind to something else."

"What should I think of instead? The two little beings doing somersaults inside you? This is for them, don't you see? Maybe you learn to look away as you get older. But I know—anyone can see—that if we don't change the way we treat not only one another but also other species, the world will keep getting darker and more dangerous. The poor and so-called minorities will continue to populate the jails and sit on the electric chair. Women will keep getting raped and beaten; gays will be attacked, murdered. And the murder of animals will continue to be the most invisible of crimes. Don't you get it? It's not just a question of changing policy but of slowing down the heart, like in the freezing chambers they use for the ectoderm, even if it means coming close to death, so the heart can change and finally open."

Hazel continued. She closed her eyes and spoke very slowly but lucidly. "You have to go deep down into your own sadness to hear the cows speak—the cows who are the pale ghosts of the buffalo. And not just the cows—coyotes, owls, eagles, ducks. Any animal. You have to slow down this end-of-the-twentieth-century time, time between seeing and forgetting, between hand to mouth, hand to weapon, thought to action, between feeling and forgetting how to feel. You even have to let go of the buzz of being human, of the way all the mirrors fill you up like a good wine that in the end really only makes you a bit tipsy and tired. In the morning it's gone, and you're reaching again for a hand to hold and a mouth that can say, I see you. You have to forget that and remember the instant when a hand holding a knife, a needle, a gun, punctures skin, and a life is ended. You have to think about it and think about it and think about it. And you have to look into the eyes of that creature and the next."

Hazel opened her eyes. "I'm not going to spend my life sitting and holding a candle while a few feet away students practice surgery over and over again on a dog before killing him."

"So are you going to become a militant? Blow up labs? Slaughterhouses?"

"I don't know. No. Of course not. There has to be something else."

She's twenty years old, Theo noted somewhat dismissively. She has to believe she can change the world, for a few more years anyway. She thought of Dusk sucking Hazel's finger. Why can't Hazel just leave it at that? Kindness to a few animals. Basic mothering. Then it occurred to Theo that maybe this was what Hazel was doing, following in her mind the logical consequences of this one act.

"It's our responsibility to think about factory slaughter, about institutionalized cruelty," Hazel started up again. "It's going on right now and now. We have to think it and think it and feel it, above all feel it." Her voice was cracking.

"No," Theo said sharply. "We don't. Not if it ruins our life. Now get some sleep. I have to go prepare for an interview."

Theo went to the living room, turned on her computer. Even if she couldn't do any work, the screen and familiar keyboard were reassuring. She was not in a position now to either rant or spend much time listening to someone who ranted. Hazel was right and Hazel was wrong. Having children meant she must accept that the world was at least to some degree a beautiful and hopeful place. It was this she had to think about, not doomed animals.

She hoped, wildly, to finish her degree before the twins were born. The hope was wild because she was finding it harder and harder to concentrate. No sooner had she established her topic—one that turned her stomach—than she thought of changing it to that of birthing twins. She thought about traveling with Hazel to New York. Why not? She had finished her course work. Although she had built a decent life in California and loved the mild night air more than she knew, she wondered whether it was enough to keep her. Her sense of place was fragile, the voice of her losses always stronger. For safety she whittled it down, a sense of place, to the view from one window. She could find that in New York. Theo was prone to nostalgia and now worked, not always successfully, to avoid it. All nostalgia is twisted, she thought. Your head turned back, in a vise.

She stared at the screen, skimming over her interview questions. They were dotted with the feeling of mist on her face, Gabriel grabbing her arm. Meatpackers. Once again, she couldn't get the subject to interest her. She tried to see M, and the man at the bar, as four-year-olds, wide-eyed and feeding the ducks. She opened a new document and typed,

Dear Jo.

I'm pregnant, did I tell you? I haven't, of course. With twins. I wish you were here. Do you remember our purses from Oma, my red and your green? The things that come back. I guess you never get over being children together. I want to know everything about your life and who you are now. Have you found love? Have you figured out how to stop it from ruining your life? How will I ever teach my children anything? I don't even know whether you're a mother. What color sneakers do you wear these days?

Love,

Of course she would never send this. A decision had been made—when? Perhaps when they each hid under their own covers during their parents' worst fights. Frightened as they were, they could not hold or even look at each other either during the crisis or after. To do so might have made things worse and so the sisters did not learn to band together, but only to lean discretely into the fragile proximity of the other.

*

"You see this?" The blond man lifted his upper lip to reveal missing teeth and a scar that ran from one end of his lip to the other. It looked infected, as though the wound had never quite healed.

He and Theo were sitting in Theo's office. She was surprised and not altogether pleased to hear from this man, one of the meatpackers who had hung around with Gabriel at *The Owl*.

"Kicked by a half-ton beef that acted up as we were getting them off the truck. They're not eager, you know." He explained his wound.

"No," Theo concurred. "I wouldn't think so."

B had three children. He lived with his family in a trailer park forty minutes from the slaughterhouse.

"How do you do it, then? Day after day, dealing with animals that are, as you say, not eager."

"It's a job. I don't think about it."

"It must be difficult not to think about it when the cows are right there making all that noise and ready to kick, too. How do you do it?"

"Life is difficult, princess."

Most calves are conceived on a rape rack, a contraption where the cow's legs are shackled and she is artificially inseminated. Hazel had told her this. The cow's motivation is lacking. She needs to be tied down.

"You have to be moving all the time," B said, "or you're a goner. There's no time to think about it. Everything is moving so quickly. You have no idea."

"What's moving so quickly?"

"The beef. I'm a skinner. They come down the line unbelievably fast. I don't have time to worry whether they're really unconscious."

"You mean you skin them when they're still conscious?"

"I just said, I don't know." He was raising his voice. He looked at her. "Yeah, I know they're conscious sometimes. What do you think of that?"

"What do *you* think?"

"I think it's a pain in the ass. It makes the work harder."

"Do you ever feel for the cows? Or do you ever wonder what they are feeling?" Theo stumbled.

"They don't have feelings. They're meat."

"How do you know?" Theo was irritated by his certainty.

"If you'll pardon me, doctor, that's not a real smart question. Like asking why cows don't run for president."

"Do you ever talk about your work with your family?"

He grinned, frowned. "What's there to say? Played basketball with a hog's head today?"

"I thought you—um—worked with cows."

"I've also *worked with*," he mocked her, "hogs."

I don't know what I'm doing, Theo panicked. She had the sensation of cotton in her mouth, cotton in her head. I can't believe I'm having this conversation. Levels of consciousness—how low could they get before the notion *sentience* no longer applied?

"Do your children know what you do?" She realized her questions were pointing him toward shame, as though his job were criminal.

"I barely get a chance to see them."

"Is that difficult?"

He looked at her again as though she were an imbecile.

"I'm used to it," he said, sparing her another caustic remark. He leaned back in his chair, waiting for the next question.

"What do you do when you're done with work to relax, to gather energy for another day?"

"That's kind of personal," he smiled. "Well, no, let me see. I kick a toy across the living room floor, unless I trip over it. I take a shower or say hello to my kids if they're awake. If it's been a hard day I spend a lot of time at the bar first. Then I go home and the wife's there."

Theo wanted to tell him to leave. "Do you talk with her about your day?" she asked, as though making a suggestion. She knew her questions sounded off, and that she was off, somewhere else.

"Oh, Jeesus. No. We have better things to do." He was mocking her again. "But it's not like I'm incapable of conversing. There is, believe it or not, somebody home upstairs."

Theo looked him in the eye for the first time and then quickly looked down, checked her list.

"Can you imagine working at your job for years to come?"

"Are you kidding? I don't think about it. But I do check the papers. Say, is your book going to make me rich?"

"I don't think so," Theo said. "Me neither."

He smiled. "I punch in and I punch out, and in between I'm like a machine. That's the way they like it. There's nothing going on inside except what I'm doing and trying to stay alive doing it. I don't think about the next day. It's like living in a closet."

"Can you tell me a little about your childhood?"

He rolled his eyes. "Typical shrink question," he said and was silent.

"What did your father do?"

"Nothing much except drink and beat us when we got out of line, and even when we didn't. At least I work for a living. You know, you can just write in your notebook, Typical White Trash." He looked at Theo, and for the first time she could see something there that wasn't a wall.

"I'm not stupid, as I've said. I've read a few books. My mother loved books."

"Tell me about your mother."

"She worked at the library for a while. She could sew us shirts out of anything. She died when I was twelve. It was his fault. I blamed it all on him. I had a younger brother to take care of, otherwise I would have packed up and gone. My brother was only five. I couldn't have left him with that bastard. A year later the state took us both away from him anyway, after he hurt a man bad."

"You haven't had an easy time of it."

"I don't need your pity, doctor."

"I also have—had a mother who died when I was young."

B was silent, crushing the cigarette pack he held ready.

He looked at her. "We're like the cows sometimes, aren't we Doctor Theo, like the big stupid animals that see the hurt coming, but there ain't nothing in hell they can do about it."

*

"I'm sorry. I was too hard on you." Theo found Hazel reading on her bed. "Nonetheless, my bed is not a sofa."

"Anyway," she went on, "it's just that I don't always want to hear about it. Nobody does. There are people who've been through worse than the animals, or as bad, and they don't harp on it constantly." She was thinking now of B.

Theo lay down on the bed next to Hazel, tired and grumpy after her interview, and felt, for the first time, a baby move. She put her hand over her abdomen, and there it was again: a small, powerful butterfly flapping its wings. Next to her, in a stack by the bed, were books about birthing and twins and baby's first year. An equally tall stack next to it was dissertation-related; books about violence, about trauma and dissociation and about the meatpacking industry. Theo was now engrossed in her research. Her chosen focus, which she felt had chosen her, fascinated, as it had from the moment she watched the videos at the farm with Hazel, and at the same time repulsed her. What interested her, too, was how the subject had chosen her—the way M and then Hazel and Gabriel had come into her life. Absorbed and then repulsed again, she wavered between a sense that she was going far afield and the conviction that she was discovering her own angle on a particularly difficult occupation.

Hazel said, "I'm leaving soon. Are you coming?"

Hazel had seen her father. She'd received no apology or blessing. She was free to go.

"I don't know." Moving seemed like way too much work, yet Theo knew she'd come to rely on Hazel's company and had a difficult time imagining Hazel leaving without her.

She got out of bed and went into the kitchen to find yogurt and oranges. Hazel had tried to get her to eat soy yogurt instead, but Theo reacted to it with even greater revulsion than to the artichokes. Wisely, Hazel did not press. Theo worried that only one baby had moved. There would be a stronger and a weaker, inevitably.

Birth

10

Theo looked up and down her empty street. It was a street dreaming itself at six a.m., a few lights like isolated notes in music not yet fully written punctuating the darkness. She handed Job, in his carrier, to Hazel so that Hazel could put him in the car. She said goodbye, just by noting them, to the sandbox, the three battered palms in the courtyard, the corner market where she used to buy tampons, beer, tuna—things she'd forgotten at Whole Foods, last-minute things. She looked at the windows of her apartment where she had led—she felt now—a solitary and provisional existence. And yet it had been hers. Her nausea was gone. Almost midway through her pregnancy, she was just small enough to get behind the wheel.

Theo moved the car through the quiet streets to the accompaniment of Job's protests. She had done everything she could to assure his comfort: bought an extra-large carrier complete with new catnip toys and treats, administered a dose of homeopathic tranquilizer, put on a tape she thought he would find soothing, made reservations in motels that accepted pets. But Job yowled and clawed at his cage unabated for the first hour of the drive, and it wasn't long before Theo was unable to distinguish his cries from her own anxiety.

She was now a mother-to-be of twins, driving across the country with a young woman who, every time she saw a truck on the highway, pictured animals inside on the uncomfortable journey to their end. According to Hazel, Hazel's mother said she was welcome to stay with them until the babies were well settled in the world. There was plenty of room. Theo wondered what this meant in terms of time— how long did it take to settle babies in this world, and to do it well? And didn't Hazel's mother think it odd that Hazel was driving across the country with and bringing home a pregnant friend, not just for a short visit but to give birth? But she couldn't expect Hazel's mother to be ordinary.

"Only the trucks with holes are carrying live animals," Theo tried to reassure Hazel. She thought this must be true but wasn't sure. Besides, what did the holes matter, really? Well, obviously, they mattered. Hazel turned up the radio, trying to disperse, Theo imagined, her focus on the animals' doom.

Santa offered scotch. Plastic reindeer were poised atop billboards. Theo thought of the three wise men moving across the desert and finding the infant, radiant in his ordinary cradle. What if the child had been a girl or twins? She read somewhere that dreaming about twins, about anything in twos, symbolized something coming very strongly into consciousness. Once she dreamt of two swans, but one was missing a head. Their necks were entwined and it was difficult to tell one from the other. She'd been in therapy at the time, but couldn't remember a thing either she or her therapist said about it. Mutilated consciousness, or more plainly, a lack of clarity—didn't most people suffer from that?

The summer Theo's grandmother took out her crèche, Johanna showed little interest in the painted clay figures and ran off to play elsewhere, but Theo was fascinated. She arranged and rearranged the animals, the humans, and the Baby, who she sensed, though no one had ever bothered to tell her the story, was not fully of either category. On a hot afternoon she played with the figures and then left the Baby surrounded by the animals, with the five robed grown-ups off to the side, and walked out onto her grandmother's balcony.

Her mother was napping on a white plastic chaise. Her Oma came out and gave Theo a cold soda. Theo watched her mother, noticed the beads of sweat that had gathered on her temple. Wanting to please her and to touch her, or perhaps just wanting the attention, she has the urge to wipe them off gently. She takes her soda bottle and places it there, on the tiny dew-like drops. Frightened awake by the sudden cold, her mother screams. She glares at Theo and then closes her eyes again. The exchange is over in five seconds. Theo goes back inside to the cool living room, where her grand-mother always keeps the shades half drawn. Chips of paint are missing from two of the kings' robes and from parts of Mary and Joseph as well. The donkey is missing an ear. She holds the donkey and Mary and pretends that Mary, who is a small girl fighting back tears she does not understand, is riding the animal away—where she does not know.

Theo's mother grew up looking at these figures each Christmas. They survived the war. She must have taken them when they went back home that summer because the next Christmas, the Christmas she shouted at Theo to make angels with her, the crèche was set up at the foot of their tree.

Theo stopped every hour or two to stretch, as the doctor had advised. Job grew quiet and she feared it was a sign of despair. Dusk came early and quickly, and she suggested they abandon their plan to drive during daylight only. They were in a gas station in the middle of a small town in Nevada, across the street from their motel, painted pink with Christmas lights surrounding purple shutters. It didn't have AAA approval, but it was written up in her guide as pet-friendly.

"What are we going to do in this town from four until ten o'clock tonight?"

"Anything we want," Hazel said. She was glad just to be out of the car.

The nothingness of the town reminded Theo of her childhood environs, of the almost row houses and her family inside one of them, fingering safety but ever unable to grasp it.

"Anything except get a decent meal, see a good movie, hike in the woods. I could go on."

"You have no imagination, Theo."

"I can imagine how depressed you're going to get when we walk into the one diner in town and try to order dinner."

Hazel was enamored of the sensation, unfamiliar to her, of arriving in a strange place only to pass through it.

"We've got plenty of our own food. Well, let's take a walk around anyway. You're supposed to walk. Besides, Job has a reservation here tonight."

They walked from one end of town to the other, up one side of the street and back the opposite side. Hazel was shivering, and so Theo handed Hazel her coat. One of the best things about being pregnant was that she was almost never cold anymore.

She had been right. There was one diner in town. Hazel stared at the coffee the waitress automatically poured into the scratched white mug.

"Just try it," Theo taunted.

Hazel looked at the plastic menu and began to read: "Dead cow part. Dead pig part. Dead bird. Animal secretion."

Theo laughed. "Come on. Contain yourself, Hazel." She laughed and yet was embarrassed by how easily she was embarrassed and then paranoid. Her mind ran without trouble to Hazel provoking someone into pulling a gun.

"I'm just decoding the menu."

"Well, do it a little more quietly."

The waitress came over. "What can I get for you ladies? For the three of you?" She looked at Theo and winked.

Theo's visible pregnancy sometimes aroused smiles, sometimes looks of suspicion or contempt. She was with a woman. She wore no wedding ring. When the response was friendly, Theo was grateful. She wanted to protect her relationship with this unknown person and felt all the more strongly that Hazel should not offend.

"What do you have that doesn't have dead animals or animal secretions in it?"

Theo winced. "She means vegetarian."

"No, I don't. I mean what I say. I want a misery-free meal."

"Look, hon, I don't have all day. What'll it be?"

When Hazel said nothing, obviously waiting for an answer to her question, the waitress walked away. A moment later a man walked up to their table.

"What seems to be the trouble?"

"I just want to know what you offer that doesn't have dead animals or animal secretions in it." Hazel spoke in a friendly, if overly intense, tone.

"Would you shut up," Theo said between her teeth.

"Well, you can order like everyone else or leave. The menu is right in front of you, ladies. I assume you both can read."

Theo tried to catch the waitress's eye. When the woman finally did look at her it was with such disgust Theo felt as though her babies had been hit. She got up and walked out the door behind Hazel.

"It's Christmas Eve," Hazel said. They sat in the restaurant adjoining their motel somewhere in Colorado. "Maybe I'll call my mother."

Theo remembered the four Christmases alone with her father and siblings before she and Johanna moved away. Half-hearted meals, her mother's empty rocker in the corner. The increasing brilliance of Martin's music. What had it been like for Martin, alone with their father after his sisters moved away? She had never gone back to find out. It was pleasant to be nowhere on Christmas.

"What's your craziest Christmas story?" she asked Hazel.

Hazel held her cup of tea and looked past Theo, out the window.

She remembered the family walk they took each Christmas morning, through the woods and then back along the road. She could remember what it felt like, to have a parent on each side of her. Why were people given two when it seemed so rare that two stayed?

"We never did much. We enjoyed the concerts on the radio and putting a few lights on the blue spruce. A tree in the house is pagan, my father said. And what's the point when we have them all around us. One year we decorated the barn. Maybe that was the craziest. We got it into our heads to decorate the barn—not my mother's studio but the empty barn. And not with just a few lights but until it was completely covered. It took a long time. We had lights we got at a garage sale one summer, and my mom gave us one strand she'd saved from when she lived alone. We wanted more. So we went to the nearest department store and bought many more boxes of lights. Just one more, he kept saying, like a little kid. Draping them over the roof took the last bit of afternoon. When we were finished we stood and watched them blinking, changing the color of the snow. That was his last Christmas with us."

"He's a bastard for not calling," Theo said. They had not mentioned Gabriel since leaving California. He hadn't

126

called to say goodbye to Hazel. Even her own father, she assumed, would have done as much.

"He can't help it, Theo. Tell me about your Christmas."

"It was the Christmas my mother and I made angels in the snow. We were in our pajamas, and when we went back inside we took a hot bath together."

Theo sees her mother's blood as if it were yesterday, on the white porcelain tub. She sees it the way she'd seen it many times in dreams after and then the way it actually was, not quite as dramatic. The blood was sparser, the silence violent as the act itself.

What she told Hazel wasn't true. It was a confabulation of two separate instances. She did remember once taking a bath with her mother; she remembered her mother's large body sliding into the tub and the water level rising. It was her most memorable lesson in physics. The angels, however, were another story.

"It wasn't like that," she said to Hazel. "Let me try again: She ran out into the snow naked. I think it was to get my father's attention."

When he was angry, at least he gave her words from his mouth, broke his ridiculous silences. Or maybe it was just hormones; she must have been newly pregnant at the time. The neighbors! he shouted, and she shouted back, Oh you, this is a country of prudes. Come on out, Theo. It's Christmas; let's make angels, my angel.

"She wanted me to come out with her. I was seven and a half years old. I did want to go out and make angels with my mother. But I wanted her dressed first. I was not tall enough to get her clothes off the hangers properly. I had this thought and then heard my father shouting, Go to your room, Theona. I want to make angels with Mama. I stood up to him. Get into your room, he insisted. You're old enough to know better. I don't need two crazy females on my hands. "

Theo tried to imitate her father's voice, to make the story funny. She moved her hand across the table, the way he'd moved his through the air in his effort to be rid of her, and knocked over her water glass. Ice cubes skated across the Formica table. The waitress brought over a rag and began soaking up the spill. Theo saw the small girl peering out her window to see her father dragging her mother in from the snow. The girl thought it strange that she could hear her mother crying through closed windows. Only when she fell back on her bed did she notice it was Johanna under the covers, whimpering like a puppy.

*

On Christmas morning Theo woke up looking into the green eye of a small cat knit with indigo yarn. She turned her head and saw, not Hazel, but the same eyes belonging to an identical cat, in red, propped on Hazel's unused pillow.

"Merry Christmas," Hazel said. She was sitting on the floor in half lotus position, reading. "For your little beasts. I knit them myself. From cotton yarn."

"Thanks. I didn't know you knit."

"I went to a Waldorf school for a few years. Everyone learns to knit."

These were the first gifts Theo received for her children. The two little cuddlies were waiting for them now, so the babies would have to come out breathing and with arms, hands, and fingers to hold the cats, with a healthy heart and brain each to love them.

"Theo." Hazel spoke, still looking down at her book. "Let's take small roads for a while."

"Are you kidding? We'll never get there."

"We have five months." Hazel tried to joke.

"Right, I'll just pull off the freeway and into your mother's driveway and start pushing."

"I'm sick of the highway. Please. Just for a while."

"All right. For one day, at the most. But let's do it when we're a little further along. You'll get tired of the lights and the strip malls fast anyway."

"No. We'll find somewhere else, another road."

"There is no other road, Hazel. You're dreaming."

Sometimes Theo found the dullness of the interstate soothing. At other moments it was excruciating, its repetitiveness slowing down time, unduly prolonging her pregnancy.

One day slipped into the next.

Hazel stared out at the long, straight highway and looked for beauty. From a distance and a certain speed almost anything could be beautiful. The wires making clean lines against the sky, the flat land with the isolated shapes of trees jutting out, even the cars passing had an elegance to them. Her mother's parents died on a road like this, further east, but on a road like this. Newly arrived immigrants, they lost their lives in an instant; her five-year-old mother, in the back seat, had miraculously survived.

They were now driving through Nebraska, through snow-covered prairie. In spring, green and yellow grasses would be waving under an enormous sky. In spring Theo would hold her babies under the same sky defined, in upstate New York, by mountains and maples.

Theo put in a Mozart tape for Job.

"You're staring," she said. Hazel had developed the habit of staring at what she referred to as Theo's baby pouch.

"I like imagining myself curled up there inside you."

"You can never go home again," Theo smiled.

"I can't understand why a woman would choose to have a baby. Not today."

"I didn't choose to have a baby. I'm choosing to have two." Theo had come to resent how the common parlance of pregnancy suggested one baby. It was like sexist language, to her sensitized ear. "Anyway, I know you're going to start about the state of the world and the animals. Let's have it."

"The babies of these babies might not have air to breathe," Hazel obliged. She sat up straighter and then slumped way down in her seat, knees on the dash. Most nights lately she could hear their screams (and, yes, they were screams) before she went to sleep—if she was able to sleep. If she wasn't, she'd still hear them, an assembly line of screams. Slow down, she would mouth to the darkness. If people could slow down their eyes and ears to see what is kept hidden behind the blur of constant movement and self-interest, to listen for what has been silenced by the whir of keeping too busy, Hazel was sure the heart, the open heart could be born, could be borne.

"Do you think I don't think about it?" Theo was suddenly angry. "Having children is not a rational decision. In my case it wasn't a decision at all. It was about as well thought-out as your desire to curl up in the womb. What—do you want to do away with people as well as farm animals? Who'll be around to enjoy this life without suffering that you envision?"

"No."

"Well, then, what do you propose?"

"To start, I propose a system in which a modest number of domestic animals are kept to produce manure for gardens and to provide company."

"As though that would solve everything—or anything, for that matter."

"I said, to start. And it would change more than you think."

"Well, that sounds nice. But the world isn't nice."

"Imagine the rosary," Hazel said. "Think of each bead as the face of a cow just before slaughter. Or, if you prefer, think of each bead as the face of a child who goes hungry because the grain that so-called food animals eat to feed a few people could have gone to feed many people."

"I'm not even Catholic."

"All right, then substitute your index cards for the beads, or your sister's postcards. Or street signs. Anything. Just think about it."

Hazel drove the small roads. Theo napped. It would be irresponsible to drive this far and not go see one. The words repeated themselves in Hazel's head. They were approaching Iowa, where Hazel was sure they would find one. It would be irresponsible to drive this far and simply pass by, without bearing witness. But a large slaughterhouse would not be found this far from the main arteries of transportation. They were lost. Hazel stopped at a gas station and called the farm where she'd taken Dusk and Patch. "Tell me where I can find one."

Theo woke from the cessation of motion. Hazel had pulled up to the gate of what looked like a top-secret military installation. "We just wanted to drive by, take a look," she was saying to the guard.

Theo rubbed her eyes. She was exhausted. Driving across the country pregnant was the stupidest thing she'd ever done, except perhaps getting pregnant in the first place. She still had these moments, when her joy at the thought of babies was overshadowed by disbelief and the sense that she was not ready, that she needed more time, another lifetime, to prepare.

"We don't allow unauthorized visitors," the guard replied. He was armed. He spoke as though he'd had trouble before, but his face softened when he looked at Hazel.

"How would one get authorized?" Hazel tried to sound demure.

"I can't tell you that. You'll have to call the office and speak with a manager."

"What exactly happens inside? We're just curious. We're tourists." Hazel was pushing.

The man waved two trucks by. Theo knew, now, where they were.

"This is a meat processing plant," the man answered. "For safety and sanitary reasons only workers and inspection crews are normally allowed inside."

"What is a meat processing plant?"

The guard looked at her, unsure.

"Tourists from Mars," the man muttered. "Listen, honey, I don't know where you're from, or what you want, but I don't have all day."

"Sorry," Hazel smiled. "I won't take any more of your time. I just thought maybe you could tell me what meat processing is, seeing as I don't know."

"We make meat here, Red."

"You make meat?"

Theo was sure the guard was putting on his slowness and tolerance because of Hazel's looks. That face and hair, her youth, were their protection. Still, Theo was nervous. The guard was probably in his mid thirties, handsome in a brutish kind of way. He had a walkie-talkie and revolver attached to his belt.

"What is meat? How do you make it?" Hazel pushed one last time.

"We make it out of red-haired girls who eat tofu. Now out of here." He put one hand on his belt.

"Would you mind if we turned around and parked long enough to check our map?"

"You have five minutes."

"Thank you," Hazel said. "You've been very helpful."

Hazel took out the map and pretended to look at it.

"You've lost it," Theo muttered. "Again." She hated it, the familiar feeling of being with someone who'd crossed that line.

It was midmorning, a brilliant sun climbing the wide horizon. Snow covered the grounds in patches, but there was no snow on the building. The heat coming from inside had surely melted it. Another truck went by. Theo caught glimpses of eyes, noses, hide.

"You can't do this to me."

"This is not about you, Theo. Just go back to sleep."

Hazel watched the truck and saw the large black wonder in the animals' hearts thumping: fear-why; fear-why; fear-why.

"No. I'm driving. You're not getting behind the wheel again."

"Don't speak to me as though I were a child."

"You *are* a child."

Hazel got out of the car. Theo feared she would run toward the slaughterhouse, but she just came around to Theo's door. Theo got out and heard the guard shout at them.

"Out of here—now."

Theo put her hands over her head and shouted back, "We're just changing drivers. Don't shoot. I'm pregnant." She could hear the guard laugh.

Theo began driving down the narrow road.

Hazel's eyes were closed.

"There is nothing to be done." Theo said the words softly, words that came without her thinking them first.

They were, she remembered now, the words the emergency medic had used to describe her mother.

They were the only and last words she remembers hearing before they took her away.

There is nothing to be done.

*

Animals do not or cannot commit suicide. This has been refuted but is still generally held to be true.

*

After returning from Mexico, Gabriel lined up gardening jobs for each day of the week, entering again the world of soil, plant, sun, and water. At the end of a day's work he let the garden hose run over his hands, the back of his neck. He stayed away from the bar. He gave himself over to running (why had she not run with him?) and dinner with Martha. The food they made together tasted good. Sex with her was like a gift someone leaves at your doorstep for no particular occasion; it was nothing he needed or expected, but certainly not something he would refuse.

He carried on like this for a while before the weight was on him again. Something worse than darkness that burned at the back of his eyes, his throat. For relief, he thought of Theo standing with him on the pier, felt again her lips brush his eyelids. He thought of Hazel spying him as he was bent low to his own feet. He could no longer remember whether he had embraced her.

11

After thirteen days on the road, Hazel and Theo drove up the long, plowed driveway into the winters of Hazel's girlhood. Theo was now, for the first time in over a decade, in her home state. Here Theo, Hazel, and Petra would settle into daily life together, three women and an unseen fourth and fifth person who were silently determining the shape and length of Theo's stay.

Hazel took Job, still in his carrier, and led Theo through an enclosed front porch. A neat row of shoes stood next to a very large pyramid of wood. Theo had never seen so much wood indoors. They walked into the house and up the stairs to Hazel's room. Petra was working in her studio. Nothing, Hazel said, will get her out of there before seven o'clock. The house smelled of burning wood, even in Hazel's room, which was small and felt like a child's room, with knickknacks and shells and rocks lining the shelves, posters of wild animals, a few postcards tacked to the closet door. A photograph of a lily, nicely framed, hung just above the simple wooden bed. Next to the bed was a clock radio with two dolls made of pipe cleaners leaning against it. The dolls faced a photo of a young boy who, Theo could see, was undoubtedly Gabriel. A large orange cat lay curled at the foot of the bed. Job hissed. The cat opened his eyes without alarm, confident.

"I'd like you to meet Nolan," Hazel said.

"Nolan, this is Job and Theo."

"In that order," Theo couldn't help saying.

"I'm afraid you're going to have to give up your room to our guests for a moment." Hazel picked Nolan up and carried him into another bedroom. "I'll let you rest," she called back to Theo. And I'll bring up a litter box and some water and check on the guest room. My mom's probably gotten it all ready for you."

Job did not want to leave his carrier. Theo lay down on the worn, clean quilt, happy to be on bedding that didn't smell like stale smoke. She was exhausted and feeling off. The previous night she'd dreamt that she started menstruating. The quilt was a beautiful pattern of greens and blues, good colors to accompany a child to sleep each night. This was a home, but not her home. Pregnant, she should be nesting, washing sheets and baby clothes. She was an aberration. She was very comfortable.

Finally Job left the carrier, paced, and snooped until Hazel returned. With a small mew he hopped into the litter box immediately and let out a long stream of pee. Theo could hear this and then the sound of his tongue lapping water before he jumped onto the bed and placed himself exactly on the spot that moments before had belonged to Nolan. From then on, Job claimed Hazel's bed, and Nolan's particular place on it, as his own.

Theo looked up at the cracked white ceiling, then closed her eyes and began to reconstruct her own childhood bedroom. She and Johanna had matching twin beds with white headboards on which their mother had painted yellow and red flowers. When she was about eleven, Johanna tried, using a thick black marker, to turn the flowers into soccer balls. When their mother saw the blotches her flowers had become, she burst into tears. Johanna could only make her sad, never angry.

The carpet was blue. It was the sea where they played sailors in spring with the windows open, the wind a sea breeze and she and her sister mates setting out on their chosen adventure. When things were good their mother would play ship's cook and bring them a tray of snacks. When things were not, their journey was over quickly, sometimes before it even began, and they were scattered like two or, if Martin was playing, three small animals in a twister.

Martin learned to sit up during one of their voyages. Theo put him on the boat, which was her bed, and instead of lying down he stayed, as if stuck, in the sitting position, his back straight as a nail, his baby grin wide enough to connect continents. He learned to sit en route to Africa—or was it India?—and, like good sea captains, she and Johanna documented it. Theo feared her mother would get angry when they told her, angry that she'd missed something. But she laughed the laugh that could go either way and said, "I suppose it's no fun lying on your back all the way to India."

After Theo woke from her nap, Hazel took her around the house and to the large barn, empty except for Gabriel's goat. The goat butted Hazel's stomach gently and then a bit harder. "He wants to play," Hazel said.

Theo sat down on a straw bale and Hazel sat down in the dirt, leaning against a wooden beam.

"What was he like? I mean the babies' father."

Theo shrugged. "I hardly knew him. Good sex, though, and he wasn't a sociopath."

"Really, what was he like?"

"Irrelevant," Theo snapped. They, too, would look beyond her. He would create a growing empty space in their lives, at the center or the periphery.

"How will you manage, Theo? You know I won't, I mean, I can't always be around. There's a lot I have to . . . "

"Don't be stupid." Theo cut Hazel off. What did Hazel imagine was expected of her? "You asked me to come here. When I think about it, I don't really know why. But I'm going back home soon after the birth. As for managing—that will be the fun part."

She would stroll with her babies across the Golden Gate Bridge. They would see poppies in February, redwood and eucalyptus, abundance. Theo idealized the place she'd decided, somewhere between Nebraska and New York, was home, far from the coast her parents had landed on to carve out a patch of chronic unhappiness.

Theo closed her eyes and breathed in the sweet barn smell. She imagines facing the Pacific and a broad, clear horizon. She sees a figure fly down from sky to water, breaking the line. It is a bird, hunting. Beyond is the inaccessible curve of earth speaking to her now of continuance, of faith.

"Maybe they can call you Aunt Hazel. It will be nice for them to have a young aunt."

Over the next several months Hazel began, slowly, to fill the barn. She did not go back to school but instead got a paying job with an animal advocacy organization. From the veterans there she learned quickly how and where to find potential refugees—those fallen off trucks, left on dead piles in stockyards, castoffs from neighboring, failing farms. She had fun naming them. The cow and calf she named Golden and Arches, the chickens were named after planets, the one-legged rooster she named Sun.

Hazel commuted to the city for her job as well as to attend various meetings and demonstrations. Often she'd come home very late, sometimes not at all. When she got home early enough, she liked to cook dinner for her mother and Theo. Sometimes she sang made-up lullabies in her clear alto voice to the babies. Hazel felt calmer now that she was working. She stuffed envelopes, made signs, and strategized. She participated in protests, egged on by a belief that the story could be rewritten.

Theo continued working on her dissertation, index cards piling up on the desk of the guest room, which became both her bedroom and study. After two months went by Theo's project once again felt remote. It was too grim. *There is nothing to be done.* Why had she chosen something so grim? She was happy wandering from one room of the house to another, noticing the way the light fell through the windows and how they framed sections of the large maples, bare and magnificent. She would go for long walks through the fields and woods, despite the difficulty of moving her growing bulk through deep snow. Petra and Hazel pampered her, and sometimes she saw herself as a patient in a nineteenth-century sanatorium, luxuriously approaching the end of a long convalescence. If she didn't fall asleep in the snow, lost on her mountain, if she didn't die in childbirth or from loneliness, she would emerge new and robust.

It was an evening in March. Theo and Petra had just finished dinner. They sat by the fire as they often did, to read and talk. Petra always spoke slowly and deliberately. Theo had liked her immediately, the first time she saw her walk into the kitchen from her studio, a dark, steady woman with a look of quiet surprise on her face. Petra never spoke about her work, but when Theo asked her about her beginnings as an artist and how she chose to work with stone Petra answered, "Stone chose me."

Theo told her how she envied her, knowing her passion so young and sticking with it.

Petra sat very straight in her chair. Like Hazel, she was tall, with generous, broad features. She had an olive complexion and shoulder-length brown hair just beginning to gray. Her eyes were a shade darker than her hair. Her hands, too, were large, the fingers long and joints swollen from the arthritis that Hazel had told Theo about but Petra never mentioned. This was the woman Gabriel loved enough to marry. Theo had no trouble understanding why.

Petra told Theo about the car accident that killed her parents.

"From one day to the next, at age five, I had no world left. All that was left were the gray slabs on which I could trace the textures of their names. For a short while after the accident I was indeed blind, a form of shock reaction. I spent hours sitting between the two stones, one hand on each. My foster parents discouraged me. I suppose they thought I was prolonging my suffering. You have to snap out of it, they said, as though I were a branch temporarily bent back. They didn't understand: Broken. But I was an obedient child and began spending less time at the cemetery. Instead I collected smaller stones, brought them to the new house that was supposed to be home, and showed no one. I slept with the stones, under my pillow, under the sheet, clenched in my fists. They kept me alive. My work is mostly a gesture of gratitude toward my material."

Theo listened. Unlike her mother, Petra did not speak with a German accent.

Outside a few flurries were beginning to come down. She had a sense of déjà vu, as though precisely this pattern of snow against starlight combined with Petra's voice had already occurred. It probably hadn't, though it might have—they'd had many nights now sitting in their respective chairs, with a fire and, sometimes, snow. Or perhaps it was caused by the fact that as she spoke with Petra she was permeated by a feeling that was deeply familiar, if only because long hoped for.

"But you seem like a very together, clear-minded person. Maybe more so than anyone I've met."

Petra smiled. Her eyes were warm, motherly. "It's true—in many people self-protection passes for wholeness. Maybe the difference can cease to matter."

They sat in silence for a few minutes, the snow gathering force outside. Petra got up to get more wood, then put a log on the fire and sat down again. Theo was aware of a slight feeling of panic she'd had when Petra got up—a fear simply that she would leave the room.

"My mother," Theo began and stopped.

"My mother killed herself when I was fifteen."

Theo did not break down, as she'd feared she might whenever she imagined telling anybody. On the contrary, she felt light, almost as though she might float away, a small boat on large waters.

Petra leaned forward and put a hand on Theo's knee. Theo could see tears filling her eyes.

"I'm sorry."

"I had to learn," Petra continued, "that the accident that killed my parents wasn't my fault."

Now Theo cried and said in a voice barely audible, "she had three children."

For many minutes, they watched the fire and sometimes the windows being carpeted slowly by snow.

"Let's have some tea and play a game of scrabble," Petra suggested finally.

Theo took the game down from the shelf while Petra made tea. She put the board on the small table between Petra's rocker and her easy chair. Theo wondered which of the chairs Gabriel had preferred. She hadn't thought of him in days and now found it difficult to picture him, especially him sitting here in either chair. Theo shook the letters, enjoying the clicking sound that they made inside the fabric. Petra, she assumed, had sewn the blue cotton bag for the wooden squares. Every single possible word is in here, she thought, and was, like a child, amazed by that fact.

12

Just a few hours from where Theo walked in Hazel's woods, Theo's father lingered in a nursing home. She didn't know he was dying until Martin called to tell her. "I've said goodbye," he told her. He was interrupting his concert schedule and could not stay to witness the arrival of his new niece and nephew or to visit. "Of course not," Theo said, yearning to see him and thinking dying must outrank birth. "Come back another time," she said. "Come to California, where I will live."

It occurred to Theo to visit her father while he was still alive, but she found she didn't want to. It was refreshing to realize she had nothing to say to him, that she and not his death would determine when things were finished. Instead she would go to the suburb she grew up in, to see her old house and visit her mother's grave.

Theo was too big now to drive, so Hazel agreed to go with her. They would leave early and visit the grave first and then the house. After, they would continue on to the city to spend the night with a friend of Hazel's. Hazel would go to her job the following morning while Theo did whatever she wanted until it was time to drive back.

Theo had not visited her mother's grave since their father took all three children shortly before Johanna left for Germany, yet she had no trouble finding the plot in the small cemetery, located on a rise about thirty miles outside Manhattan. The partial view of the city's skyline mimicked the stones in an odd way. That summer when she was nineteen some of the stones were covered with seagull poop. Now they had thick, neat loaves of early spring snow resting on them. More snow was accumulating, heavy and slow, as they came to a stop in front of Astrid Mueller Eaton's stone.

That earlier time, in summer, when her mother's death and her sister's immanent departure turned somersaults in Theo's stomach, Martin brought his violin. "I want to play something for her." They were all relieved not to have to stand there in awful silence. Martin took the violin out of its case and began to play, his skinny arms slightly reddened from sunburn, the left one holding still except for his articulate fingers, his right arm both following and guiding the bow with awkward grace across the strings. Their father had his head in his hands; Johanna was looking off into the distance like a runner to her goal. Theo cried for her mother, for the music she had loved disappearing into the muggy air, and for the few hearty trees dotting the otherwise barren hillside. She cried for the music played by the frail-looking boy who she loves so much and who has also, in his way, left her. She cried, of course, for herself.

They stood in front of the stone in silence, the snow falling around them, Theo's babies feeling big and kicking inside her. Hazel's presence began to irritate her; she didn't want her there, just as she didn't want her nineteen-year-old self there, breaking down under the loveliness of her brother's music. She wanted to be alone or with someone older, Hazel's mother, perhaps, someone who could better understand. And of course she wanted *her*—she could begin to feel it now, how she wanted her back.

"She was very good with you, you know, when you were babies. A very good mother." Theo's grandmother wrote this to them shortly after the suicide. Theo ignored the letter then, but the words came now and she leaned into them, conjuring her mother's hands holding her small, hungry face. Love navigating through curves of palm, finger, cupping her cheeks as though they were two warm peaches; it must have occurred at least once.

To stand in front of a mother's grave filled Hazel with fear and a numbness that began to relieve the fear. "Never go anywhere," she had made her mother promise the first time her father was, as Petra put it, lost. And her mother did promise, but perfunctorily, without looking at her. Hazel put her arms around Theo and, when she felt Theo stiffen, stepped back.

Theo stood alone repeating, silently, the word *forever*. The word was at least something, but forever itself, what was it? Snow that would never melt to reveal grass, a thirsty tongue not ever reaching water. Her mother was forever nothing, dead. And now she filled the world. She was inside Theo; it was like that, as if she were inside like the babies, but forever. *It was for the best. It was a mistake.* Voices after the fact. What did she find when she got there? Had she kept the ring on to ease her journey? Or because she meant to live? And now her father was going, too. All the years he had continued to live, and Theo had barely spoken with him. She looked around for Hazel and found her close by, sitting under a large pine. She thought for a moment about joining her, about huddling and hibernating there with her strange friend until—until when? But she reached out a hand. It was time to go.

They drove up to the house, just a house now, with a stranger's car parked in the driveway, and stayed for only a few minutes. What else was there to do? It was repainted a different color; the new car was not the old VW Bug. Snow covered the square patch of yard just as it had twenty years ago. The neighborhood had become more expensive. Every house, including this one, had an extension or two added on. This and the years shrunk the yard.

Theo got out of the car and stood on the side of the road opposite the house. The street had been a place then, a place for playing war, house, hide and seek. She had learned to ride a bicycle on this street, though she had a clearer memory of Johanna learning, soaring down the hill after their father let go of the seat. She looked at the square of snow and could see precisely the spot where her mother made the angel, close to the house. A security sign was planted there now. Armed response, it read.

"I think I want to go see him."

"Who?"

"My father."

"Good. Yes, I think it's a good idea."

Her mother had, she presumed, loved this man once. They'd had three children together. There must be something he could tell her, something she didn't know and that would make a difference, something she could pass on to her children.

The nursing home, not far from her old house, was not a fancy one. Had he retired early or lost his job before becoming ill? What exactly was wrong with him? She realized she didn't know. She didn't know when he'd gotten sick, when it had been determined he was dying, when he'd been moved here. This was a holding pen, with the assumption visible everywhere that these lives, preparing to end, had no need for anything that might be considered extra; certainly there was no need for beauty. How surprising, then, to find—after walking past room after barren room, rooms where the television came closest to anything living— that her father's room had a plant and a bouquet of flowers in it, both placed carefully so he'd have full view of them.

When he turned to face her, she could see the familiar bitter expression, now watered down with the vagueness of the very weak. She saw the hint of a smile.

"My big girl."

Was this a reference to her pregnancy? No. He was simply referring, as he always had, to the fact that she was his oldest child.

"I am truly big now." She tried to draw attention to the fact that he would be a grandfather soon. He didn't get it, so she stepped closer and said, "I'm pregnant."

He saw and an expression that was childlike and without greed spread across his face. It was an expression of delight, gone just after she registered it.

He darkened, and she knew he was thinking of *her*.

"Just don't ever leave your children. Or your man."

"Why? I mean, why did she?"

Theo sat in the chair near her father's bed and began to tremble with relief. She'd asked the question held in half her life.

What could he say to this woman, his child—the one who most resembled him? His voice, when he was able to speak, seemed so far away. He was moving closer to her mother now. He would have a chance to ask her. Perhaps she would turn on him, or put her head in his lap as she used to do when they were young and newly together. He could stroke her hair, admiring her long neck, the childlike curve of her cheek. He would feel again the pride of bringing home his beautiful German girl. And then he was floating above it all again, above his life and memories as though looking down on a quickly passing landscape from an airplane. He was inside this fast-moving vehicle. He would never be able to touch anything or anyone again. Shapes of countries, of bodies, objects, of the golden retriever he'd had as a boy. And then she took it, like a dog a bone. She took his hand.

If I had loved her better. Maybe if she hadn't lost so much during the war. She had an illness. He could say that.

Theo could see he was not going to answer her question. She could see the question had written itself on his face without answer, without possibility of erasure. This was his answer; this is what he was showing her. Her hand moved to the slight tremor of his hand.

Had the kindness always been there? In this man who'd bought his son a violin? Who would not accompany his wife to the graves of her brothers?

"Who sent the plant and flowers?"

"Virginia."

"Mom's friend."

"Yes."

He shut his eyes now, exhausted from talking. The nurse came in as if she knew, and said, "He's like a baby, just falls asleep when he's tired. Blessedly peaceful compared to some." He'd let his hand slip from Theo's, and Theo placed it at his side.

*

Hazel opened the door to the organization's office, and Theo was greeted by a panoramic photo of several cows caught at various stages between being themselves and becoming meat. They hung upside down, in a messy row.

There can be no peace among people until the violence inflicted on other animals is recognized and shuddered at within each human heart and therefore ceases.

These words were stenciled onto the wall in large letters, to the right of the photo. *Eases*—they could have written that instead of *ceases*. Theo longed for what was possible. The room had a bookshelf, a few cafeteria-style tables and chairs. A young man sat at one of the tables, stuffing envelopes.

"Hey, Hazel," he said and looked up briefly.

"Sam, I'd like you to meet Theo."

Sam looked up again and smiled. He was probably eighteen or so, blond, very pretty.

"There's a demo at noon," he said to Hazel. "In front of White Buffalo.'"

"OK. We can make a few signs."

There was no one else in the office, and Theo wondered whether Hazel and Sam would be the only people at this demonstration.

Hazel walked Theo over to the other table, which was covered with animal rights literature as well as popular magazines and newspapers in the process of being cut up. On the far side of the table were the cut-out images, some already pasted onto signboards or pieces of paper.

"We are re-membering the animals, untwisting them from, or reflecting back, the perverse place they have been put in this society," Hazel explained, sounding like something she'd read. "We make these placards and display them in highly visible places. We ride subways or stand on the platform; we park ourselves outside delicatessens and health clubs. Buses are good because there's nowhere for people to go."

Hazel went over to the wall where some larger pieces of paper were rolled up and brought over a huge collage with a drawing at the center of a cow and her calf, the calf suckling. Two close-ups were juxtaposed, showing the young one's lips around her mother's teat and then the cow looking directly at the viewer.

"I didn't know you could draw."

"I can't. I did the collage. Sam did the drawing."

Sam was in art school and said he finally felt like the work he did was good for something.

"And this?" Theo asked, putting her hand on a large binder. When she started to open it Hazel stopped her.

"Those are plans for a long-term project. I can't really talk about it without Diane's permission." Hazel's subservience and secrecy surprised Theo, especially given the way Hazel had spoken of Diane.

Diane and her husband John were the leaders of the organization and the ones paying Hazel her small salary. Diane had a lot of heart and even more money, which she used to start the organization and buy acolytes willing to do things her way. People loved Diane because she so unabashedly put herself at the center, the beautiful baby no one was required to pick up or diaper but simply to admire. She was zealous about her work, truly feeling for animals. And she gave a lot of parties and gifts, to make sure people would be there when she needed them.

Hazel began working on her signs and Theo sat down to look at some of the literature. There were the usual photos of the unspeakable, accompanied by verbal descriptions. How anyone could read more than a paragraph at a time, she did not understand. She read and paused. Read some more. As when she watched the videos and did her research, she was drawn to knowing, but less so now, growing more sensitive, insular, the further along she got in pregnancy.

"I need to exercise these babies to sleep."

"Right," Hazel answered without looking up.

Theo walked down Fourteenth Street feeling oddly calm and safe, her steps jiggling the boy and the girl gently. She carried them like some new knowledge from block to block, warm inside her coat. She cherished her visible breath, the feel of her enlarged breasts, and a delirium of hormonal sureness that amounted to a temporary damming up of everything she could fear. The streets were crowded with people and merchandise despite the weather. She rummaged through a table containing scarves, a box of old postcards, a basket filled with Chinese cloth shoes. She could find only one tiny pair and so decided against buying any.

On the other side of Washington Square she found a café, ordered a decaf coffee, and began making a list: *diapers, undershirts, hats, blankets. Changing table? Money*–underlined twice. Petra offered Hazel's old crib, which they still had in the basement. She supposed the babies could take turns— the one who didn't have the crib could sleep with her.

Theo picked up a newspaper someone had left at the neighboring table. She opened to a large ad featuring two Lord and Taylor mannequins drawn in charcoal, displaying spring fashions. Above this was a small article about genocide in Rwanda and another about the death of a child at the hands of other children. She put the paper down again. Do things, she wondered, keep getting worse? Or do they just repeat in different forms? They do repeat but the forms grow more menacing. That was plain. Or was it? She made two columns. Boys' names underlined. Girls' names underlined. *Martin* headed one list, *Johanna* the other, though she knew she would not use them. *Hazel*, she wrote, *Gabriel, Petra. Astrid* and *Edward. Miguel.* She had shortened Miguel to M, even in her own mind, because that is how she referred to him in her research. Writing his name now she could hear him speaking it the first time they met, could remember the sound of promise in the foreign accent. But no, she would find names to give her children a fresh start.

She herself had been named after her paternal grand-father, Theodore, who died before she was born. A photo of him as a youngish man had hung in her father's study, and she'd mistaken it for her father until he pointed out to her that this was the grandfather she was named after. When she'd asked why she was not named after a grand-mother, he said only, because he was a soldier and a poet.

Her mother had come into the room just at that moment, and said that she had wanted to name her after Oma and that her grandfather had not been much of a poet. To avoid the argument she could sense brewing, Theo did not ask anymore questions and left the room.

Dear Jo, she doodled on the back of the lists, and then, when nothing more came, folded the paper and tucked it away.

When Theo returned, Hazel, Sam, Diane, John, and a few others were preparing to leave for the demonstration.

"Which sign will you carry?" Diane greeted Theo.

None, Theo wanted to say back, but didn't. She would do this for Hazel, once.

White Buffalo had evolved a decade earlier from an exclusive men's club into one of the city's most expensive restaurants. Theo stood reluctantly to one side of the revolving door, its polished brass frame reflective as a mirror. She wore a sign with a drawing Sam had done (from a photo) of a goose being force-fed. A tube almost as thick as the goose's neck was plunged down into the bird's throat. *Your appetizer is my torture,* the sign read. It was lunch hour. A limousine pulled up and a bald man and a woman in a fur coat got out. The woman looked at Theo and the other demonstrators. She walked by Theo, and Theo was sure the woman would spit at her. It was surprising how clearly Theo could see this. The woman was going to spit right into her younger, less compromised face.

Diane noticed Theo step back, away from the woman.

"You're new at this, aren't you? I was doing a lot of demonstrations when I was pregnant. I know what that's like." Theo had not imagined Diane having a child.

"It's herself she can't stand," Diane continued. "Look, she's wearing these dead animals on her back. She knows somewhere inside that it's wrong. That her wealth is all wrong. She's bored with it, not to mention with herself. In an hour or two she'll emerge glassy-eyed. I grew up around this set. So I know something. Just remember: anyone can change."

"I should be home knitting booties," she said to Diane. But Diane had already moved to another spot, busy handing out leaflets about veal production.

A manager from the restaurant came out and threatened to call the police if the demonstrators did not relocate. Diane pointed out that the sidewalks were public. "You are loitering, blocking customers' entrance and exit," the man retorted. It was the usual exchange. Diane had obviously been through it many times. She told the group to keep walking up and down the sidewalk a few blocks on either side of the restaurant. Theo wore her sign, her fetuses thrusting the force-fed goose at passersby. The sidewalks were dense with traffic. The sign had become her skin, too thin, and it made her feel as though she were naked in an inappropriate place. She was sure she would bump into that one person waiting to make headlines, to blow up. What would it be like to actually see anger, hatred, envy as shapes, colors, smells in the street? She longed for Petra's rocker by the fire and her calm, slow voice.

Hazel was walking ahead. Theo saw a man stop her and begin a conversation. He was in fact conversing with Hazel's sign, since it was a body sign she had wrapped around herself, with two holes for eyes and one for her nose. There was no opening for the mouth, only a drawing of a fish mouth pierced by a hook. Around the mouth was the caption, *Any sensitivity here?* She and Sam had made the sign together, with the intention of her wearing it. The images were just the right size to fit and be seen clearly on various parts and angles of Hazel's body. Theo wondered whether

Sam did the drawings while Hazel was wrapped in the paper. She saw such a peculiar moment of intimacy between them as she watched the man talk to the hooked mouth, and to the two green eyes, whose beauty he could not have overlooked. Maybe he was coming on to Hazel, aroused by a tall woman or man (her sex would not have been revealed until she spoke) papered with animals at various stages of mutilation.

The group walked back and forth, toward White Buffalo and away. A homeless man peed onto one of the straggly trees that lined the street, not just opening his zipper but letting his pants fall around his ankles. A hotdog vendor recently parked laughed at the demonstrators. Could he read their signs? A woman with three children in the back of a new green Land Rover pulled up near the little cart. She double-parked and ran toward the vendor, who took her money and squirted mustard on three—three what? Theo was no longer sure what to call them. The letters M and B should be in there, in the name, she thought. There was a little bit of those two men, of both their stories, in that product.

13

Hazel watched as Theo crossed off another day on the calendar.

"Let's go out into real time," Hazel said.

They stood, three women making a semicircle under the star-filled night. Theo looked at Hazel's profile as she lifted her head to the near full moon. Hazel began to sing. The contours of her face became for a moment one with the constellations, small points of light in the sky. If the stars could sing, they would sing like this. Theo loved Hazel now as her child, as though Hazel's bones had taken shape inside her, and she feared for her the way she could only begin to imagine fearing for her children, for the way a single sunrise could vanquish even—especially—those who sing.

Hazel's voice cracked and she was silent.

"What is it?" Theo asked.

Hazel put her hands on Theo's belly.

Indoors, Theo had warm soymilk; Hazel and Petra had tea. Carol, the midwife, would be coming in the morning for Theo's biweekly appointment. Theo finished her drink and went upstairs to her room, craving time alone, away from Hazel's intensity. She began to organize the index cards strewn over the desk and bed. Hazel's old dollhouse sat in a corner, near the desk. White with bright trim, it reminded Theo of a birthday cake, not the kind her mother used to make—lovely marble cake with powdered sugar sprinkled over it—but the traditional American kind you could order at any bakery, full of butterfat, sugar, and food coloring. Hazel told her it was a gift from Gabriel, a misfired apology for forgetting her fifth birthday. And where are the dolls, Daddy? Hazel had asked. He had not thought of that. Quickly, he made some dolls out of pipe cleaners.

Theo put her cards in a pile and thought about making a house out of them.

The babies were a good size. The first had her head down; the other was breech, but that was common, and he would probably somersault before birth.

"You're only a month away, Theo. The babies could be born any day now." Carol spoke to her after the examination. They sat at the kitchen table. After a while Hazel and her mother joined them.

"Do you feel ready to be present when Theo births her children?" Carol asked Hazel somewhat ceremoniously, as though asking Hazel to confirm her vows.

Carol had been present at Hazel's birth as an apprentice midwife and had remained a good friend of Petra's.

"You know, it's a bloody affair," she put it bluntly, having seen too many well-meaning friends faint. "Not always pretty. You'll see your friend in some pain. Although," Carol stopped and looked at Theo, "it will be pain Theo can bear, and she will do fine, bringing two beautiful children into the world."

Hazel looked out the window. The lawn and maple leaves were at their greenest after an early morning thundershower. She loved that green. It reminded her of her father, touching a longing she resolutely no longer paid attention to. Nonetheless, she could still love the green. There was great freedom in that and in savoring the wet grass between her toes, the leaves dripping when she stirred them.

"Sure," Hazel answered Carol. "What's a little blood?"

Before Carol left, all three women lay their hands on Theo's belly. This was a ritual Hazel had initiated after Carol's first visit. Theo barely tolerated it. So New Age. Hazel had that flaky side to her. And yet Theo came to appreciate the attention. It probably was good for her babies, taking (or beginning to take) whatever hurt sat in her body up and away. She looked down at the six hands making a giant star on her globe-shaped uterus. The babies' hands plus her own: they too made six. Theo noticed Petra's large, long-fingered hands, knobby at the joints, and Carol's smaller, softer, thicker hands, hands that looked more conventionally middle-aged. And there were Hazel's hands, the hands of a child by comparison, strong, but still unmarked.

The women sang, and Hazel listened to her mother's voice. It came back, the sound of that voice as she sat on the dirt floor playing with pieces of stone while her mother worked. Why had she always thought of her as working in silence? It was this: they'd both listened so hard for his voice that her mother's predictable humming became indistinguishable from the ins and outs of their waiting.

Theo saw Petra also observe their hands. How quickly the hands change. For her the change, the first softening of the skin must have been superseded by the crippling, slow at first and then quicker each year, until it affected her work, forcing her to leave the stone be and preserve the simplicity that proved, eventually, to be its heart. The heart and fate lay side by side, strangers at first, but gradually coming to recognize that their arranged marriage was held together, after all, by love.

*

On May 3, exactly one week earlier than the calendar predicted, Theo's first baby journeyed through parts of herself she would never see and emerged unscathed, her head pointy as a magician's hat. Interminable seasickness and pain and there was Claire, a wise baby from the start, taking her time before drawing that first breath, and before moving toward the breast or anything outside of her old, forever ruptured world.

Hazel held Theo's hand. Petra wrapped Claire in a blanket and held her while Theo continued to push. When Hazel let go of her hand and said something unintelligible in a high voice, Theo panicked. The second—the breech— the weaker. She would not know if the heart had stopped. Perhaps her pushing was hurting him. What did Hazel know?

But it wasn't the baby. Hazel must have caught a glimpse of him standing near the door. When Theo saw his face, shortly after Claire was born, and as she was preparing to push out Simon, she thought in her exhaustion she had made him up, a father for her children, and then that she was seeing her own father, looking as though he might fall over, drunk. "Get him out of here," she said.

His timing this time had been impeccable, impossible.

Petra had let out a small cry when she saw Gabriel standing in the doorway, unshaven, tired, with the face of a vagabond, a lost child. She had gone to the kitchen to get more ice cubes for Theo. It was a face, she knew immediately, she would tell Theo much later, that she could still love, but would only pity. It had been almost six years.

"What are you doing here?" The words came just barely, dry and choked.

"They asked me to come." It was a lie, but Gabriel believed it to be true. He looked at his wife. She was the picture of his failure to love.

Petra did not believe or disbelieve him. He was too late. He would always be too late. She looked at him and said it. "You're too late. Go away. You don't belong here." She looked past him to an outside that seemed surprisingly unchanged. It was a spring morning. A butterfly sat and fluttered in the driveway.

She could see his face cloud over with the child's sadness and shame that kept her from hating him. His fine gardener's hands hung at his side with nothing to do. Touching them had become impossible.

Petra held the screen door open. When he did not leave, she did not shut it and did not invite him in. He didn't know whether to go or stay either. He'd been asked to leave. But he could not.

A loud moan from Theo sent Petra running back into the house and up the stairs. Gabriel moved inside the doorway, letting the screen door close behind him and leaving the door ajar. The stairs were not far from where he stood. He could hear Theo's grunting and the sound of quiet talking. He recognized Carol's sure voice. Hearing her, even more than seeing Petra, brought back that moment he had missed, returning to find his wife alone with their new daughter. The disgusted look Carol had given him when she returned to check on mother and daughter. He could still feel that.

Standing in his house, what had once been his house, he felt Hazel's childhood and his marriage close around him the way he imagined his father had felt his absent limb. He could still hear his father saying in his alcohol-changed voice to his mother, "You've only got a broken man now. Better get yourself a new one."

Gabriel walked up the creaky wooden stairs, stairs he had never thought to wish into silence all the nights he returned late. He moved quietly past the birthing room, what had once been his and wife's room. The door to Hazel's room was open and he went in. His lack of contact with her made him sentimental. He remembered everything in her room, which looked almost unchanged since he'd last seen it, except for Theo's cat. Job jumped off the bed when Gabriel stepped in and ran from the room.

The photo of a lily, which he had taken and framed, still hung over Hazel's bed. Her posters and postcards covered most of one wall and the back of the door. A few had fallen off, leaving circles of scotch tape here and there or dark outlines where the tape and cards had been. He imagined her room used to be tidier. The painting she did in school of young turtles moving toward the sea was on her dresser, leaning against the wall. Although the turtles were misshapen, the painting had power in it. Baby turtles are born on the beach and then, not long after they hatch, find their way to the water on their own. She had told him this. Or had he told her? It was this fact, it seemed to him, that she'd painted—the deep, subtle blue of the water pulling the small creatures toward it, their barely visible legs taking them where they needed to go.

On her night table was a photo he did not recognize. It was a photo of a boy at eight or nine years old, standing in front of the vacant lot where he and his mother used to pick blackberries. Liam's uncle must have taken the photo. He was an amateur photographer, the only one in the family with a camera, and had taken many photos of the family and of community events. Once he took Gabriel with him to a large Polish wedding where Gabriel was allowed to eat and drink as he pleased while his great uncle took pictures. In this photo he is looking at the camera, not because in it he imagines a reflection of himself or because the person behind the camera is someone he wants to please. He is, he remembers now, wishing himself through the lens into another world—a world that he, in his child's mind, is struggling to see.

He looked out the window. The two large maples still stood, even bigger now, between the house and the barn.

Petra's studio was up the hill a bit and out of sight. He turned again and looked at Hazel's bed. He remembered the wooden crib they'd found in good condition at a yard sale, and that had stood in the bed's place until Hazel was almost three. The dollhouse was missing, but two of the pipe-cleaner dolls he'd made sat next to the clock radio on her night table. Petra always thought the dollhouse an ugly, extravagant reminder of his failings as a father. He had not forgotten Hazel's birthday—fourth, or was it the fifth?—he just didn't remember it on the exact date. Time flowed in such a rush he didn't understand how anyone could keep up with it, pinning it down, as though it were a piece of cloth or a dead butterfly.

The sound, like an animal in pain, was louder than anything that had come before. He had to go now. This much he knew. And he knew he was afraid, of what he might see and what he might not see.

He walked toward the room and Theo let out another long grunt, followed by a wail. The door was still open, but he did not dare go in. He could see Theo squatting by the bed, Petra, Carol, and Hazel hovering around her. Hazel was facing the door. She was very pale and looked like she might fall over, as though it were she who was in pain.

"It's time to push the second baby out," Carol said firmly, but with a trace of shattered calm in her voice. Theo heard this. Took it in, like a needle into the tenderest skin.

A loud groan. And then, she wanted to give up. Only this. He could not see her, only little bits of her back and shoulders, her dark hair soaked with sweat. Second baby. Was there more than one? Petra was right; he didn't belong here. He was spying. He felt ashamed and yet couldn't leave. There was something here that he needed, and it was love, or something like love, that brought him.

"That's great," Carol said. "I can see your baby's head. Bring me the mirror, Hazel."

Hazel reached one long, wobbly arm to the bureau and retrieved a small hand mirror.

"Do you see that head of black hair? That's your baby, darling. You're doing great. Now push your second baby out. The baby needs to come out now."

Theo had the sensation that her womb was an ear into which Carol poured her words. The words swam with her remaining baby, a part of him, apart from her. She pushed until she felt she would explode like an overheated fruit. Then she felt a head pop out.

She must have pushed two more times (for she gave two more groans), and then he saw it. Theo was lying on the bed now. Carol was holding the baby. Hazel moved to the side just at that moment, as if to let him see a purplish thing covered in blood, immense and tiny at once.

Blood and silence. Gabriel was seized with nausea. He could not stand alone outside the room anymore. He entered and stayed, amazed by the grip with which fear and love could arrest him.

Theo looked at the small circle around her, without really seeing anyone. She'd seen her baby boy for just an instant, lying, perfect, in Carol's arms, with the umbilical cord tied neatly around his neck. There'd been a moment of silence, as though everyone had joined Simon in not breathing. *Call the ambulance*, she'd heard Carol command while she moved quickly in her efforts to bring him breath. "You're hurting him," Theo shouted loud and long until she could no longer see anything but the wanting of this one life, this darling life, so bright before it went black.

Theo, still half in a faint, held Simon, while Petra held her, until the ambulance came. Carol held Claire, and when Gabriel asked to hold her she nodded and, somewhat reluctantly, passed the infant to him. Hazel sat in a chair in a corner of the room, looking like a sleepy, stunned child. Gabriel walked toward her, Claire hidden in the quilt Petra had managed to sew. Simon was also, now, wrapped in his quilt. Gabriel stopped when Hazel was within whispering distance. She came to and looked up when he said, "I think we should leave the room for a while." She got up without speaking and followed her father into her bedroom. They stood, awkwardly, looking from the infant to Job, so as to avoid looking at each other. When Claire gave a short cry they both looked at the yellow and pink bundle. "Hazel," he looked at her now. "It is you I have come to see."

They heard the sirens and the commotion but sat on the bed and did not move. After, when Carol came in to retrieve Claire, they went outside to the barn to see the goat. Exhausted, Hazel told Theo later, they eventually both fell asleep in the straw. They did talk, but exactly about what Hazel never did say. When Hazel woke up, he was gone.

*

Claire was nursing. She could do this.
"This hurts. Breastfeeding hurts. Everything hurts."
"Not for long," Petra assured. "I mean the feeding."
"I cannot do this." Theo was weeping.
"This is the most difficult time."
Tug suck tug suck tug suck.
Two perfect faces, true as mountains, and now only this one wanting her breasts, and—how could it be—she felt angry; Claire was hurting her.
Theo knew Claire was in danger. She might live in the shadow of her brother who Theo would have to love in a

way she could not love a living, growing, vulnerable child. She looked down at her surviving child, protective.

Petra said she'd seen the look in his eyes each time he looked at her and they said, I will be leaving again. And so before he could say it, she said, "You should be going." He was sitting on a straw bale beside their sleeping daughter. It was late morning and she'd come into the barn looking for Hazel. Petra was pleased she had had the chance to say this, what she would never have said, never, six years earlier, but again his leaving took her by surprise. A normal person would have waited until Hazel was awake, but he must have walked out of the barn shortly after she did, and down the length of the driveway, eventually sticking out his thumb. The length of his absence now, Petra would say later to Theo, about equaled the length of time she had been given with her parents. Of course, if you put them on the scales, each set of five, almost six years, they would not weigh the same; the scales would not balance. Her first five years so light she barely knew they existed, and the five years without Gabriel, heavy and then empty, by turns.

Hazel went back to work, longer hours each week.

When she wasn't in her studio, Petra helped with the baby.

Claire was sleeping, a month old now and fully cherubic. Theo was able to sit and walk and pee again without pain, and Petra had been right, it no longer hurt to nurse. She was tired as usual this afternoon but did not want to nap with Claire. Instead, she sat in a chair in the bedroom and read, and then watched her daughter's breathing as she wondered when to tell Petra she would be leaving. She needed to get back, finish her degree, and figure out a way to earn money.

Her mind spun. She could never leave this chair, the summer sun warming her through the open window, the promise of conversation with Petra and Hazel. She was closer, geographically, to Johanna than she'd been in years. She could visit. Or Martin, she could visit him. But they should be visiting her . . . Where was everyone? Why did her father have to die, now, just as she'd recognized his decency? Theo could feel her eyes closing . . . Sleep came heavier than ever these days, but it never lasted long. Hers was the sleep of the night watchman.

Work

14

Hazel worked long hours for Diane's organization, so it was Petra who fed the animals and called in the neighbor's boy to muck the barn. Petra often lingered in the barn, rhythmically smoothing the sides and back of the ailing Golden, or Kuh, as she called her. The soft hide and flesh over bone spoke to her, in a way she could bear, of children leaving.

When Claire was just over a month old, Hazel traveled with Diane, John, Sam, and a handful of others to the Midwest, to begin implementing the long-term project she had been so secretive about. It was Hazel who suggested they go to the slaughterhouse she and Theo had stopped at briefly the previous winter.

"I know one of the guards there," she exaggerated.

Packed into John's old van, with Diane and the children following in her Volvo, they left Manhattan and began driving west. Hazel was dedicated, but being on the road again felt wretched. She already longed for the woods around the house and to be alone rather than crowded in facing back seats with Sam and the five others, though she liked Sam, liked his body and the way he always smelled fresh as a child after a bath.

The trip took two days. Diane knew an activist who lived an hour away from the slaughterhouse. The group could camp there for as long as they needed to. Diane, John, and their two children would rent a separate apartment.

The plan, roughly, was this: they would gain access to the grounds of the slaughterhouse, not to the inside right away, but to an exit where they could catch the workers before they drove home or to the nearest bar. The group would invite the meatpackers to a meeting in which other job opportunities would be discussed. Food and drinks would be served. The organization had, with Diane's money, already bought a nearby hundred-acre parcel of land and several smaller parcels, which they intended to use for organic farming. A few farmers agreed to attend meetings, train workers on their farms, and help get the new farms started. Those who came to the meeting would be invited to join the project for pay at first equal to what they earned slaughtering, but to increase as the farms became productive. These small produce farms would grow to eventually include cooperative daycare, a farm store, and an education program as part of the operation. Over time, when the anticipated decrease in slaughterhouse labor was felt, each farm would also house some of the swelling number of surplus animals. The plan would start slowly and as quietly as possible, becoming more visible as popular support and the farms grew. This was Diane and the groups' vision. They predicted the plan might take ten years to gain momentum, over which time they would buy more land, and infiltrate more slaughterhouses.

It will never work. You people are completely naïve. Think you can take on major corporations as well as the fast-food-eating populace.

Hazel did not have to tell anyone to hear the voices. They were in the air. They were right. Yet she was excited, hopeful about the plan. Still, more drastic measures were needed. A part of her believed this. She will disappear, she thought. We've all got to disappear. Come back different. Yet change would come slowly, through work as repetitive as stuffing envelopes, skinning cows. Both these facts were true.

She remembered her conversation with the guard, the tall, blond guard with the kind of blue eyes that chill if they don't arouse. She imagined his robust, probably hairless chest, and something—some imperfect, vulnerable spot—that would make him feel real under the brown uniform.

They met at the bar where the white workers hung. Diane agreed, reluctantly, to Hazel's plan to seduce the guard. She agreed it might be useful, especially once they wanted access to the kill floor.

"Be careful; protect yourself," she told Hazel.

Sam was Hazel's first lover and they were good together, meaning happy. Hazel did not discuss this plan with him; it did not occur to her.

Charles was no fool. He looked at Hazel from across the small table in the bar where he drank beer and she drank soda water.

"What do you want from me?"

"I don't know," Hazel said, looking directly into his eyes. She was curious about him. She'd found him right where he'd been when she and Theo had driven away.

"Why'd you come back here?"

"I quit my job and am trying to figure out what to do next. Whenever I pass through a town, I try to visit with anyone I know. Maybe I'll get some ideas."

"How old are you?"

"Twenty-one," she replied, adding a few months to her age.

"Yeah? I wouldn't have guessed you were that old. Legal."

His icy eyes turned on her. "I hope you left that animal rights shit back east. 'What is meat?' Give me a break."

Hazel nodded.

"Well, Hay – zl," he dragged out this first syllable of her name with obvious enjoyment. "I have only one thing for you. I could teach you that." He grinned. It was not a nasty grin, but one that said, OK, let's have a good time.

They developed a routine of meeting at the bar, where Hazel would watch him down three or four beers. He told her his job as security guard had been hard won. He was one of the few workers who stuck it out on the kill floor for years. His fifth year he was knocked unconscious by a cow that had not been stunned properly. When he came to, he threatened to get a lawyer. That was when they offered him his current position. Better pay for less work; job security and benefits. He couldn't turn it down.

Sometimes they played darts before they drove, in tandem, to his trailer. Hazel always drove herself there and back again, using one of Diane's friend's cars. After they'd known each other a few weeks, and the group's meetings were drawing about twenty people each time, something changed between them, quietly, like a wind changing direction. He started drinking a little less. He turned the light on when they entered his place and offered her something to eat. He said he wanted to see her face while they made love. He used those words, *make love*, and Hazel grew uncomfortable. But now was her chance.

"I want to see where you work," she said. They sat in the tiny kitchen of his trailer eating chips and salsa. Hazel looked around, nervous now. There was nothing on the walls except a small crucifix and a pin-up girl calendar.

"You already know where I work," he replied.

"I mean I want to see the inside, where the animals are."

"God—why? It's horrible." He looked at her suspiciously.

"Then how can you keep working there?"

"I never go inside anymore."

"But you know what goes on. Never mind. Can you take me in, just once, please?"

"No. I don't want to do that to you," he added, looking past her.

"Please," she appealed.

"What's the matter with you?" He was getting angry, then caught himself and said again, "Let's change the subject. I thought you left that stuff—have a beer for once."

"No. Thank you."

"Come on." He set a beer down in front of her and leaned back in his chair. She noticed a tattoo on his left shoulder that resembled a dragon, but she wasn't sure. She didn't want to look too closely.

"No, I don't want one." He looked at her and she looked at the opposite wall.

"Interesting choice of wall ornaments."

"Hey, you watch it . . . Don't you go insulting Jesus or the forms his Father put on this earth."

He smiled. "Give me a picture of you and I'll pin it up."

"Maybe, if you . . . "

"Oh no. I make the deals here. I'll tell you what. If you drink a beer—no, two beers—I'll let you onto the kill floor. You can see all the blood and guts you want."

Hazel was quiet for a moment. "Are you serious?"

"Cross my heart."

Hazel lifted the beer to her lips. She did not put the bottle down until it was empty.

"Wow," he said, and chuckled.

He put the second beer in front of her and she emptied it, too.

Hazel's body floated into each corner of Charles's kitchen. Her forehead felt light, as though it were a separate chunk of matter. She had the urge to laugh, then to cry.

When Hazel left Charles's trailer that night they agreed to meet the following evening a half hour before the end of his shift.

"The slaughter will have just started up again," he told her.

Diane gave her a small video camera. "Take as much footage as you can, and don't get caught."

The idea of filming the animals' agony and mutilation was repulsive to Hazel. "Just another undercover video of a slaughterhouse that only the people who don't need to will watch." Hazel showed Diane a rare moment of cynicism.

"No," Diane said. "Not *just* another. Another. And to have another is important. Repetition is important. We need as many of these as we can make. Our goal is, of course, to have the videos shown widely, on network news, for example. And I think we can get there, especially if the footage has a strong movement behind it, a movement whose effects the general public is beginning to notice."

Inside her head, Hazel had been in the slaughterhouse so often, so intensely, that following Charles into it now was almost like following him into his trailer for the tenth time. It was familiar, if not entirely comfortable. She was not afraid.

Once inside, however, it was a nightmare.

She turned the camera on before entering and had the lens peeking out between the buttons of her canvas jacket, which was black like the camera. She followed closely behind Charles, her eyes focused on his back.

Later, for her first film, she would splice in texts, quotes from other witnesses, and footage from feedlots and stockyards. Throughout the film there would be the recurring image of Charles walking, getting further and further ahead of her.

Outside again, she began to shake. She expected someone to grab her, but there was no one. Even Charles had disappeared, probably not wanting to get caught himself. Sweat opened her, everywhere. It would never be over. There was no waking up. There was only inside and outside. She'd been inside probably less than fifteen minutes. It was still light out and it hurt her eyes to look at the empty white sky.

Over the next few weeks she forced herself to go inside, again and again, to get more footage, to touch an animal one last time, until Charles's love for her or their luck ran out.

He did not know, though he began to suspect, that she was talking to the workers during their short breaks, convincing the most reluctant to come to meetings, promising money and a future. He did not know she felt the world shrink with each animal killed, and that she felt her insides grabbed by the gloved hands and her hair torn out, because this was no place for beauty. She felt she must add something of her own to the discards bucket, because the degradation of one life is the degradation of many. The foreman saw it, its unexpected color there, where there was usually only blood and guts red, brown, black, purple. And she, much later than she should have been, was caught.

15

When Theo mentioned to Petra the idea of going to Germany to see Johanna, Petra said, "Yes, you must go." She even offered to help pay for her ticket.

"If I had a sister, or anyone left there, I would go," she said. Theo felt the sweep of Petra's loss.

"I couldn't do that," Theo said, referring to the money.

But Petra insisted. Her work was selling well. "I would like to do this for you."

Traveling alone with an infant seemed insane. "Will you come with me?"

Petra shook her head. She had not heard from Hazel in over two weeks.

Theo sent Johanna a postcard proposing her visit and received an immediate reply on a card depicting a tourist boat on the Rhine. *Yes, come,* was all it said. Below this, Johanna's signature and a postscript giving a phone number. After buying her ticket, Theo left a message on a machine that had a German man speaking words she could not, for the most part, identify. That language, like the feel of her mother's hands on her face, had almost disappeared from memory.

Theo imagined a trip that could be distilled onto five postcards. One for each day, not including travel.

The first postcard shows a functional, postwar apartment building made of concrete and painted a dark gray with white lines around the windows. Each apartment has a small balcony. A blue umbrella on one of the balconies and a few flower boxes add color to the picture. If you look closely you can see a woman standing on the sidewalk. She is looking up, one hand pushing a stroller.

On the second card the faces of two women, each squeezed into the frame of a passport-size photo.

The third card shows a castle that sits on a hillside. The left half of the Schloss is in ruins—only the fragments of two walls remain. The other half is in good condition, with curtains on the windows and a green awning jutting out to the side. Under this awning are several white tables and chairs and two café umbrellas.

Card number four shows the hillside on which the Schloss sits from a different angle. One can make out the small street that winds halfway up the hill before the vineyards swallow it. Along the street are three houses, each with an orange clay shingled roof.

The final postcard is of a young girl wearing a yellow dress. Her hair is in braids and she smiles, biting her lower lip. There is no background other than a cloudless, colorless sky.

Postcard #1

The language. The stewardesses and some of the passengers spoke it and now in the airport it boomed over the loudspeakers. Words here and there suddenly familiar again, as though a passage had been cleared, like her ears popping.

The feeling of arrival and, simultaneously, return. It came back, this feeling she had absorbed through her mother's skin. Finally, we are here. Not in our one fragile nest, but among the elasticity and safety of the tribe. Yet there was no tribe, only her sister, who might be the tall, blond woman standing under a TV monitor.

Bratwurst turning. The smell of them that—Hazel aside— she still loved, and the familiar oval rolls split open to receive them *mit Senf*. With mustard.

Theo had to get fairly close to make sure the elegantly dressed woman was Johanna.

Johanna stared and said, "My god, you didn't mention a baby!"

"This is Claire," Theo responded, trying to ignore Johanna's tone, which indicated the surprise was not altogether welcome.

They could not fully embrace with Claire, who was strapped to Theo's chest, between them, but brushed each other's cheeks lightly and then stood apart.

"I can't believe you're here."

"I can't believe I'm here either."

A heavyset woman wearing a floral print dress was mopping the staircase of Johanna's apartment building. "Grüss Gott." The woman muttered the traditional greeting. She straightened, but did not look at them as they passed. Johanna mumbled a greeting in reply. Theo remembered this from visiting her grandmother—always a woman like this mopping the steps.

They took the elevator. Had she changed as much as her sister? Johanna wore tight white linen pants, white sandals that looked uncomfortable and a well-cut navy blouse. Gold jewelry. They stood close in silence. The aura of affluence made Johanna seem older than she was. Theo was conscious of her own thrift store clothes—the dark, short skirt and worn clogs, and the yellow T-shirt with at least one milk stain on it. As a teenager, Johanna had scorned fashion. She always seemed to be wearing a uniform for one sport or another.

When they stopped at the fourth floor, and Johanna looked at her and said, "here we are," Theo knew those blue eyes, the full lips that smiled easily. Yes, this was definitely her sister; her face had not changed all that much. Maybe it was the shaft of light that greeted them in the hallway that brought back standing together at Martin's crib early one morning. They were holding hands. Each wooden bar of the crib held an unsteady piece of spruce shadow. He turned his eyes toward them and a new smile flickered across his face. Johanna squeezed her hand and she squeezed back.

Johanna set down Theo's bag and took out her keys. Her husband, Dieter, was an attorney who often worked very late, she explained. They moved down the dim hallway and, at the end of it, Johanna turned on the lights. Theo saw white leather furniture, a glass coffee table, and bookcases with glass doors.

"Here is the guest room." She pointed to a small room just off the living room. "I didn't know, so I didn't set up a space for the baby."

"Oh, that's fine. She sleeps with me." Theo wondered again whether Johanna was irritated by the fact that she had not come alone. She, also, for a moment, longed for it to be just the two of them, with twin beds six feet apart.

"However you like," Johanna said. She did not coo over Claire or remark on her large dark eyes, so different from Theo's; she barely seemed to see her.

"Claire's probably ready for bed. I'll go put her down. Then we can have some time together."

Theo put Claire, who was already asleep, in the center of the large bed and surrounded her with piles of clothes and blankets so she wouldn't roll off.

When Theo returned to the living room, Johanna stood with a glass in her hand, looking out the double doors that must have led to a small balcony.

"Claire's asleep," Theo said.

Without turning, Johanna said, "Actually, I need to go teach now."

"Oh. So you teach? In the evening?"

"Tennis. And tomorrow I work at the fitness club all day. But we'll have the evening." Johanna was facing her now.

"Let me show you the kitchen and bathroom before I go." It occurred to Theo that her sister had gotten dressed up to meet her and this, for some reason, made her want to cry. They passed through the kitchen and into a very clean bathroom that had a nice smell. "Here are some towels for you and," she grabbed another from a shelf, "one for the baby."

Johanna looked tired; Theo noticed it now, under the bright bathroom light that revealed the circles under her eyes despite the make-up.

"Thanks."

"Oh, and here's something for water." She handed Theo a red plastic cup covered with white polka dots.

"These are just like the ones Oma used to have."

"I know. Oh, and there's a key for you on the small table in your room. I imagine you will want to go to bed early. See you tomorrow."

The sisters moved a bit closer but did not hug.

After Johanna left, Theo walked out onto the balcony and stood there for a long time. The sounds and smells of the city were at once foreign and familiar. When she was very small she used to savor the song of the ambulances that passed at least once a day. Because she knew nothing, it comforted her. She caught a whiff of hops from the nearby brewery and felt, for a moment, as though she had never left her grandmother's apartment.

If she had thought about it, Theo might have expected Johanna to have freed herself up. But she was glad to have time alone. She wanted to walk her mother and grandmother's, and now Johanna's, city with just Claire first. Theo filled the polka dotted cup with water and set it down next to her bed. She fell asleep to the sounds of traffic, to the feeling of being a girl in her grandmother's apartment, while her cells hummed to the warm small body tucked under her arm.

Standing in front of what had once been her grandmother's apartment building, she imagined opening the dark cherry doors of the cabinet where her Oma always kept her best china and her Schnapps glasses. Theo could conjure the full, sweet, slightly musty smell that she'd occasionally gotten hints of elsewhere, in unexpected places, but never in the split-level ranch she grew up in. Where was that smell now? Had she expected to find it in Johanna's elegant apartment? How could it be that the blue and white Meissen china was no longer in the cabinet and the cabinet itself gone to wherever dead people's unclaimed furniture is taken? Both Theo's mother and her mother's sister, Sabina, lived overseas. They took only light things when their mother died. Theo's mother took a serving spoon, a few dishcloths, a small vase Theo remembered buying flowers for one summer at a shop near the train station.

She squinted into the sunlight. A breeze blew a series of white shirts back and forth on a balcony that could have been her grandmother's once. Again, the smell of hops. Theo remembered the attic—the place to hang laundry when it rained or when there were more pieces than the small balcony could hold. The wooden roof beams gave off the smell of heat moistened by the freshly washed and wrung cotton. They had played tag there, darting under and between sheets and clothing.

Claire was asleep in the stroller, curved toward one side. Sometimes, when she slept like this, Theo imagined she was reaching for her twin. Theo looked at Claire's face and back again at the building that had been a familiar place once. Her grandmother had lived here from the time she was widowed until her death. The apartment she'd lived in before that, when Theo's mother was a girl, was destroyed in the war. The war was a subject her mother alluded to, but did not really talk about. They were too young, anyway, to take an interest. A woman holding a toddler came out of the front entrance, a metal door framed by squares of thick opaque glass. The child held a stuffed animal, a dog, bearing an insignia Theo recognized.

"Haben Sie hier etwas verloren?" the woman asked. Theo smiled and then remembered that question. The words said, have you lost something here? But they meant, what are you doing here? Theo thought of saying my grandmother used to live here. *Meine Grossmutter hat einmal hier gewohnt.* She tried the sentence out in silence, which took too long.

"Nein," she said instead, and then, not wanting to appear suspicious, added, "Stadtbummel . . . machen wir." We're just taking a walk about town. Theo could not get the construction right on such short notice.

Theo walked the streets with the repeated sensation of not knowing where she was, of being completely lost, and then suddenly finding herself on a street corner or some other place she recognized. She found the cemetery where her mother had gotten so angry with her and where her uncles, grandfather, and now her grandmother were buried. It was a large cemetery, and she did not know how to find the grave. Again she had the feeling of an irritatingly indeterminate distance between where she was and what she was looking for. She pushed the stroller over the fine gravel down the narrow path edged here and there with boxwood. When Claire woke, hungry, Theo sat down on a bench, exposing her breast to a large slate monument and the grass surrounding someone else's dead.

Theo looked at the face whose sweetness still shocked her. *Claire. We're looking for your great-grandmother's grave.*

I wish you could have known Oma. Theo spoke softly, but audibly, to Claire. Oma had always seemed like the perfect grandmother, but in what way, Theo wondered now, might she have contributed to the fact that Claire would grow up without one? Someday she would have to talk to Claire, to tell her about her grandmother and about her brother and her father. She'd lost so much already, this infant, without even knowing it. Theo was glad it was years until that time and that, for now, they were free—or Claire was—of that knowledge. *It's you and me, for a little while a relatively simple equation, and I hope I get it right.*

"Look at this." Theo held Claire close to a big, red tulip, and Claire tried to grab it.

Theo put her back in the stroller with the cat Hazel had knit for her. She'd buried Simon's cat with him, tucked it under his tiny arm. She wasn't sure this had been the right thing to do. It was true, she had not wanted to look at it and had not wanted to throw it away either, but mostly, and of course irrationally, she'd wanted him to have company.

Postcard #2

Johanna and Theo sat across from each other, Theo on a white leather sofa and Johanna on the matching easy chair. Thanks to Hazel's influence, Theo could no longer sit on leather unselfconsciously but, unlike Hazel, she could sit on it.

Her legs stretched out on the coffee table, Johanna held a glass of the red wine they had started at dinner. Dieter had phoned during the meal to say he'd been called out of town. He introduced himself to Theo that morning, on his way out, a tall man with brown hair, handsome in a forgettable way. Like Johanna, he did not seem to notice

Claire. In any case, Theo was glad he'd be away. She wanted the time alone with her sister.

"I'm sorry I didn't come when you invited me. I was messed up." Theo wanted to get this out of the way.

She thought about it but never told Hazel about the porcupine with the mysterious wound. She thought it better to protect her friend from slipping under the skin of this one animal, at least, dying too slowly, cars swerving around it as though this were the good still left in the world. Theo told Johanna instead, as part of a vague and muddled explanation as to why she did not visit more than a decade earlier.

Johanna said nothing for a while, looking down into her glass. "My English is filled with holes," she'd said earlier.

"It doesn't matter," she said now, in English with German inflection. "It was so long ago." Then she added, "Though I had my problems, too."

"I kept all of your postcards." Theo had a dream recently that these had been destroyed and thought of telling Johanna. But she knew it was often odd, listening to other people's dreams. If she practiced as a psychologist she would no doubt have to listen to all kinds of dreams; boring dreams, disgusting dreams, horrifying and erotic dreams. It was difficult, sometimes, to imagine subjecting herself to this, to making her ears so vulnerable. It was like being a priest in a confessional. But to be a priest you have to believe you are serving God; that your ear is a conduit to God. She had believed psychology might give her a map, as in a fairy tale—a map to name the obstacles, and speak what was necessary to break the spell that prevented her from entering into her true, rightful life. The fact that the map led to studying people who kill animals for a living remained perplexing. She remembered playing Pin the Tail on the Donkey as a child. Spun around blindfolded, with the tail in her hand, and the rest of the animal somewhere in the dizzy dark, she was left, but only for a moment then, with the sensation of shoving a pushpin into air.

"Why did you do it?" Theo asked.

"Do what?"

"You know, come here. Move away. Or move back. Whatever."

Johanna shrugged. "I guess I thought I could find her here. With all the memories, hers and ours. That it would hurt less."

Theo looked at her sister. She was still wearing the training suit she must have worn all day at the fitness center. Her hair was back in a ponytail. She looked more like the old Johanna.

"Did it work?"

"No. Sometimes. Mostly it just made things worse, because I also missed you and Martin, and even Dad, too."

"Why didn't you come back?"

"I can't really explain it. I feel like I belong here. Maybe I'm still looking for clues to who she really was. Besides, none of you exactly encouraged me."

"What was it like, going to the village where Mom lived?" Theo evaded the accusation that, as far as she knew, was accurate. She thought of the card Johanna had sent depicting this village that she'd pinned on walls for so long and that was now in storage along with most of her things.

The sisters looked at each other.

"It's hard to remember. Just ordinary," she said. She did not say, as Theo knew she could, I kept seeing her; kept waiting to run into her. "I took the bus and had to wait for a long time. I didn't know what to look for once I got there. She hardly ever talked about the village, except Opa's pharmacy, and that wasn't there anymore. I tried to imagine a little girl running down the street with an ice cream or something but couldn't. All I could see was myself growing old, becoming one of the shriveled women speaking in a dialect I've learned to understand. Remember, how we'd make fun of it when we were younger?"

"Let's go there together." Theo had not expected to say this, but knew immediately that this was what she wanted to do. She wondered whether her sister had gone back again, once or repeatedly, but did not want to ask.

"I don't know." Johanna got up to open another bottle of wine. She poured herself a glass and took a long swallow.

"That was the day I met Dieter."

"In Mom's village?" It struck Theo that she had almost never used the word "Mom" after her mother died, and that she was almost getting used to it again, this designation she and her sister could pass between them.

"On the bus going home."

Dieter didn't seem like a man who rode buses anymore, but he was about Johanna's age and would have been very young at that time.

"He was a student. He'd been visiting his grandmother, who lived in the village until she died five years ago. Anyway, we used to visit her together for *Kaffee und Kuchen*. I became quite close with her." Johanna's voice trailed off.

Theo looked at her sister and noticed a certain vividness of expression that had come with this recollection, and that then faded into a vagueness that did not invite further discussion. This closeness Johanna spoke of, Theo wanted to know it, but her assumption that it was gone from Johanna's life both in fact and in essence led her to change the subject.

"You haven't asked me about the father of my baby."

"I didn't want to pry. *Ein Mann*. A man, I suppose. They're all the same."

Johanna looked at Theo and they laughed. Theo did not imagine Johanna was happy in her marriage, but she did not want to press. The truth was she did not want to hear any more sad news.

"Well, I guess so. There's not much to say anyway. I only saw him four times. He was Mexican. A meatpacker. One of my research subjects."

"You're studying meatpackers? *Ekelhaft!* Digusting. Why?"

"Well, I wasn't when I met him. I basically was operating on a vague sense of wanting to discover some pattern to unhappiness that could be traced to a precise moment of loss in childhood. Something as precise as when a vase gets broken—something with a clear before and after. Nothing very original, really. The meatpackers kind of found me, you could say."

Johanna poured another glass of wine.

"After she was gone, German lay there, demanding to be used," she said, "demanding I never lose her tongue, her country. "I have something." Johanna got out of her chair and walked to the next room. "For you."

When she returned she held out a small silvery clump. Theo took it. Johanna sat back down with her wine. "Guess. Guess what it is."

"I have no idea."

"Guess," Johanna insisted.

"A very large filling?" Theo joked.

"A piece of the Berlin Wall. I chipped it off myself." Johanna became animated and spilled her red wine onto the white carpet. She looked at the stain, and shrugged. "So what? When I went to Berlin, it was so exciting. I really felt like I was part of something. And I knew she would have been there, too. I could feel Mom with me, chipping away at that Wall with all her strength."

Johanna threw her head back and laughed a laugh Theo recognized. Wild and giddy, it was their mother's laugh. Theo felt it on the back of her neck, expecting the unpredictable slap of the unmoored. But nothing else happened except that her sister got up to clean the stained carpet as best she could, then poured them each another glass.

"It's funny," Johanna said, sitting down again, "how things unfold.

"I believed so long in a resurrection and that if you came, and maybe Martin, too, we could somehow make her materialize—here. I believed we were strong enough to do that. I know it sounds crazy. Anyway, here you are, and I realize there was some truth to my idea."

The sisters sat across from each other, and relaxed into a somewhat drunken sadness.

Postcard #3

Theo and Johanna drove to their mother's village. They walked up the hillside, vineyards to either side of them, climbing the narrow dirt path after the pavement and then the cobblestone ended. The air was getting heavier and it was hot. They stood looking at the Schloss, half of it a tumble of stones. Theo sat on one of the metal chairs, its white paint peeling, to nurse Claire. Always there was that—the small mouth hungry for her, and in exchange she got to sit, just sit and look at Claire's face.

An elderly man came through the door and said, "Das Café ist geschlossen." The café is closed.

Johanna explained that their mother was born and had lived in the village before and during the last years of the war.

The man went back inside and came out with a bottle of soda water, raspberry syrup, and three glasses on a tray. "What was her name?" *Wie hat sie geheissen?*

"Astrid. Astrid Mueller," Johanna said.

"They had the last house on this road; the house furthest from the main street. You passed it on your way here," the man told them. "I remember two older boys and a very small girl. That must have been your mother."

He paused for a moment and muttered something under his breath. "When they returned from the city, after the bombing, it was just the parents, the girl, and another girl, still a baby. The boys were off in Russia."

Sabina, their mother's younger sister, had married an Australian. This was all Theo knew about her.

"Before the war, your mother's father had the pharmacy in town. He was like the village doctor, very well liked and respected. *Verstehen Sie?*" You understand?

"And our mother?" Johanna asked. "What was she like?"

He shrugged his shoulders. "A beautiful little girl . . . But when the family returned, she was different. Half-grown, skinny, like most children during those years. *Die schreckliche Zeit.*" The horrific time.

Johanna continued to translate for Theo as the man spoke, but she was surprised by how much she could understand.

"They had given up the house, but the people living there kindly took in the whole family. Their apartment in the city had been bombed. I used to let your mother dig up a few vegetables from my garden. I didn't have much myself, you know, but the idea of hungry children . . . They stayed until the war was over. I hardly ever saw your mother in the end. There were rumors that she was ill. *Wer weiss?* Who knows? Everyone was sick, then."

"Does anyone live here now?" Theo asked. There were obviously lots of rooms above the café.

Nein. Nicht mehr. "Not anymore. Only myself; I am the caretaker. There is talk of turning it into a hotel again, as it was in the sixties. Before the war it was a sanatorium. Many people came. It was very well known.

"And where are you from? Americans?"

"I live here. My sister is American."

Their mother must have walked up the road to this Schloss, still whole then, her hand in her father's, accompanying him as he delivered medicines to the sanatorium residents. She was five when her father was drafted and they first moved away, to the city. She would have barely remembered the sanatorium, or her father's pharmacy, but enough to speak of it to Johanna, apparently. When she returned, four years later, the Schloss, the man told them, had been taken over by the Nazis and was off limits—*natürlich.* Of course.

It began to rain. The baby needed changing. The man hesitated but invited them inside. He hurried Theo through a large front room in which photographs from World War II and just before were framed. Theo passed images of the familiar banded arms stiff in the Nazi salute and of a city, probably Dresden, in ruins.

"Museum," the man said quickly.

Theo could feel Claire's poop leaking onto her arm.

Was that what this place was? Not a café, but a museum? There only seemed to be a handful of pictures. Maybe she was in a neo-Nazi fortress. Her mixed-race baby soon to be sacrificed. The poop on her arm was sliding down toward her hand. Claire began to scream. She followed the man reluctantly, Claire under one arm, the changing bag slung over the opposite shoulder.

Johanna elected to stay outside. "I love the rain," she said. She paid as little attention to Claire as possible. Was it jealousy? It didn't seem normal. But then maybe Johanna wanted children and had not been able to conceive yet, or she didn't want to have them with Dieter, who, Theo sensed, was a philanderer.

The man led Theo to a tiny room with one small oval window. It could just fit the narrow bed and a cabinet of dark wood, probably cherry, with a large ceramic pitcher resting on it, which Theo recognized as a *Nachttopf.* Literally, night pot, meaning chamber pot. Who had slept here? And did anyone use it now? Perhaps it was an old sanatorium room, though it looked more like maid's quarters for that time. She supposed an SS officer could have taken his boots off here and rested.

"Sie können die Kleine hier versorgen." You can take care of the little girl here. The man left the room and Theo turned her attention to Claire's poop. She rummaged in her bag for a dry cloth diaper and the small sheet of plastic she used for situations like this. She spread the cloth on top of the plastic and then laid Claire on top of both, on the bed. She quickly took out a disposable diaper, wipes, rash cream, calendula oil, focusing on the objects, on the motions her hands made as they unsnapped and slipped off Claire's floral jumper. She distracted her daughter with funny faces and a rattle. When Claire had calmed down, Theo took a wipe and got the poop off her arm. Claire had diarrhea; the trip was too much for her. It was Theo's fault, of course, for bringing her on this trip that she should have taken alone years ago. She did not think about the man or the swastikas, or this castle her mother must have visited as a child. And she did not think about her sister standing in the gentle rain, and the ways in which they refused to enter each other's lives. She did not think about the rain. Or about how much she did not know. Could not have known. Here was Claire, calling for her basic attention. As long as Theo did everything according to the established rhythm, to Claire this would be just another diaper change.

When she was finished, the man appeared as if by magic to escort her out. They left the building by a different door and did not go through the large front room again. Theo carried Claire across the cobblestone courtyard to where Johanna was standing and looking down to the village. She turned around once more after she put Claire in the stroller. The man stood by the door and watched them leave.

"It must have been lovely to come here as a girl," Johanna said.

"Oh, yes. The Nazis must have made terrific company."

"I meant before that. Before all that."

"It's a lovely spot," Theo agreed, sorry now to have snapped at her sister. "Where did your husband's grandmother live?"

"In one of the new apartments on the outskirts. Let's see if we can buy a bottle of local wine somewhere. This village is known for its wine."

Claire was asleep again. The half-ruined Schloss lay behind them. The sun was coming out. The sisters took off their shoes to feel the dirt and then the wet, warm cobblestone under their feet. Their feet remembered, would always remember, how it was to play together. Together maybe they could invoke their mother running here as a girl after the rain, when the vineyards gave off that smell, almost a taste, of grapes ready to be harvested.

Postcard #4

Theo noticed the roof first, because it reminded her immediately of Johanna's postcard. It was made of clay shingles chipped and faded to a warm, lazy color that had changed as much it ever would. New shingles were interspersed, bright and shiny, like false teeth. The walls of the house were a light gray plaster. Each long window had two sets of shutters: dark green wooden ones, some still shut, hung inside the frame, while fastened to the outside of the house were larger metal ones, their slats so narrow they would let in practically no light at all. The windows with open shutters revealed curtains of thick white lace. One of the windows swung wide, a puffy white down comforter draped over the sill to air. A large woman stood at this window. She stood as though she had always been there, unquestioningly, like the shingles and the shutters. Yet there had been a day when their mother had stood here. The woman was maybe in her late fifties, the age their mother would have been now. The two women might have known each other as children. Theo tried to picture either woman as a small girl skipping down this road in a loose cotton dress, running into the nearby forest to forage for edible mushrooms and plants. Her mother was easy to picture as a child. She had always been a child. But this woman was more difficult. She stood at the window and would not budge. She waved them away with what must have been a reddened and work-worn hand.

"Ihr altes Haus," Johanna shouted, with an urgency that made Theo jump back. Her old house. The woman did not respond.

Theo watched her sister turn, walk a few paces, then stop and look down as she dug with her toe into the reddish earth.

Postcard #5

They crossed the main street and walked up another small alley, past a church and several more houses. Behind the houses was a cornfield, tall and blond against the robust blue sky. Leaving the stroller, they walked the narrow path between the stalks and then crossed a small wild field, coming to a row of poplars guarding a stream. The way children will run right to water. This came to Theo. The way that particular impulse diffuses. She held Claire while Johanna spread out a quilted blanket. It looked vaguely familiar to Theo.

"I'm tired," Johanna said.

They washed a few plums and a bunch of grapes in the stream and ate them with bread and a thick, dark chocolate bar. Johanna opened the bottle of wine they had just bought. The little stream moved quickly. Theo watched the waters part for Claire's feet and ankles as she dipped them in. Her mother would have found this place, war or no war. Thrown her dress off.

After one glass of wine Johanna curled on her side and fell asleep. Theo looked at her sister, at the gold bracelet surrounding her tanned wrist and the thick gold wedding band hugging a diamond. She looked at Johanna's profile pressed against the brown and blue fabric, trying to locate the history of that blanket. She had learned so little about her sister, now and even during the first eighteen years. *Guten Abend, Gute Nacht.* She sang Brahms' Lullaby under the dappled shade of the poplars, until Claire was also asleep.

Awake, she wanted to stretch this afternoon until it reached—what? She listened to the stream for a long time, and then, closing her eyes, spoke to her mother.

You are somewhere in that sound, in the disappearing water.

I see you, a small girl wearing a yellow dress running uphill along a narrow path, almost invisible between the mature grapevines. The path is the path to the Schloss. I am watching you from the bottom of the hill, which is a world already lost to you. There is danger at the end of the path. I know this, because I know you will disappear. I try to call you back. Why don't you hear me? I shout louder and louder but do not follow. I cannot, although I want to more than anything. I know that yellow dress and it is as though I can touch the fabric, feel it precisely, because it is so familiar. But that dress came much later. Still, I believe for a sweet instant that I have brought you back. But you keep moving away. You disappear around the bend on the dusty path toward the soldiers, toward the ruin, and then, abruptly, your frightened face moves closer and closer until it is a landscape, until it is the dry cracked German earth.

I've searched for that moment over and over and can see it now, though now I also know that it is a mirage and no longer the right place to look for you.

You are somewhere in that sound, in the disappearing water.

You are here, reflecting, partially, the ways I will be able to love my child.

16

Petra's delight in Claire delighted Theo and she thought, at times, of staying. But she only planned to spend a few weeks in New York. She'd find a driver for her car and book a flight back to California soon. Petra had had no word from Hazel since she'd gone off with the group to— Hazel had said—somewhere in the Midwest. Theo tried to reassure Petra, who was clearly anxious. Hazel used to call her mother each week from California. This time there were no phone calls.

Theo soon got back to work on her dissertation. When she wasn't in her studio, Petra was more than happy to care for Claire, and it occurred to Theo that in California she would have to hire a babysitter. She was approaching her topic from two angles: the exploitation of immigrants for labor (she was trying to look at this from a psychological perspective as well as the obvious sociopolitical one), and the connection between violence and dissociation. What happens to people when they are forced (because it is their job) to kill; what happens when they are forced to kill over and over again? These theoretical angles would be the foundation of her work, and the meat, so to speak, would be ten interviews with slaughterhouse workers. She still had most of the interviews to do. The ones with Gabriel and Miguel she would probably have to throw out.

Theo was up late working when Nolan hopped onto her lap. She looked down at him and asked, "Where's Hazel?" She was worried. Hazel, she felt, was capable of doing something extreme. She could envision her trying to block trucks on their way into the stockyards or the meat-packing plants. "I am a cow," Theo remembered Hazel's words. She could see her disappearing into a dark, crowded trailer, curling herself between the legs of animals and, when the semi reached its destination, getting trampled.

She petted Nolan and thought about fear, about all the surprising shapes it took, and how its absence could open awful and wonderful doors. The phone rang. It was Diane. Petra had probably been asleep, but picked up her phone shortly after Theo answered the call.

"Your daughter is in prison. I'm sorry; but she went too far. She was careless and may have jeopardized everything we've been working for."

"I'll hang up," Theo said into the phone, to Petra.

Theo did not trust Diane. Diane was in it all for her own weird marginal glory. She would elaborate on Hazel's weaknesses and shape them to her own ends.

Nolan hopped off her lap and went about his business. At least Hazel was alive. She wasn't sure whether to go to Petra's room at this late hour, but felt it would be cold to do nothing. So she got up and walked to the bedroom where she'd given birth a month and a half ago. The door was shut and there was no light on. Theo could not hear any sounds of conversation. She was sure Petra lay awake but would not disturb her.

Prison, Hazel would tell Theo, was like being alone in the woods but without the woods and without the self that connects with the woods. From this emptiness Hazel could, sometimes, conjure the trees and the mosses as they smell in spring after a rain, smells of beginnings, resilience, tenderness. Here, there was no time and only time. Hazel indulged in long thoughts about those she loved. Of her parents, only with her mother did she have a relationship close to what she might have hoped for—a relationship that, therefore, was strangely without hope or yearning or any quality other than itself. Her mother had protected her, uncomplaining and reliable. Now she sat on the other side of the bars, the very picture of ruin—unreachable, stone. And then, after a time, she returned and softened.

"You are trying to do something good. But you're hurting yourself. You cannot hurt yourself, Hazel, and do good."

"I'll be out soon. Where's Theo?"

"She just got back from Germany."

"Why didn't you go with her?" Hazel knew her mother must have considered this.

Petra just looked at her daughter and then closed her eyes. The memory came to her of Hazel as a toddler and of how her then arthritis-free arms could encircle her daughter, lift her anywhere.

"I have something for you." Petra had checked with the officials and they'd said it was all right to give a book to her daughter.

Petra handed Hazel the copy of Russian poetry in German translation that had belonged to her parents. "It has a poem that one of my favorite poets wrote while her son was in prison. Anyway, I'd like you to have it, even if you never learn the language. It belonged to your grandparents."

Dear Sam, I am sorry I did not tell you the whole story. You really are a good friend. I hope we spend time together when I get out. I have nightmares, memories, and I wish you were here to hold me.

She was in prison only a week, but a week is not the same in prison. She wrote letters, sometimes on paper, sometimes in her mind. She had nightmares and so tried to avoid sleep. She grew a new skin. Her cellmate was in for drugs and punched her because, she said, she looked too good and too privileged.

Sam said to her, you've gone too far. When Sam visited he looked like a child. He cried when he saw her black eye. You've taken it too far, he said. And she knew he was right, but believed he was wrong. What is too far? She thought about that a lot. What would she do when she got out? What was there to do?

She and Sam could laugh together more. Her mother was in pain every day. There was Claire's completely innocent and beautiful face. She tried to remember these things, to keep perspective.

But she is in, where he'll never be, though she knows it won't be for long. Everything is gray, the air stale, and the light dim. Her cellmate was older, Latina. She is in solitary now. They'd made a mistake, putting them together. Someone said this, but Hazel doesn't know whether it is true.

This is a country she has never seen. The floors are concrete, like in the slaughterhouse. She finds herself longing for comfort, but then doesn't find herself there. She thinks of the animals. She thinks of Theo's twins, one dead, one alive. What is at the end of the road of comfort?

She has come to the end of her world. Was this the logical, inevitable conclusion to her actions? It will end soon. How can she go forward?

She says to Sam, "I will take you to the cabin in Maine. It's peaceful. Beautiful, like you."

And she will go there now without the burden of having to find her father. She has learned that what happened has happened and, more importantly, what did not happen will not. These empty spaces she can live as her freedom.

"I'll think about it," says Sam.

She feels a moment of panic, and then there it was—her freedom, Sam's freedom. What had bound her was the knowledge of cruelty and suffering, the extent to which she imagined their caged miserable lives. That was her prison as much as anything. This is her question: how can she be free now, without abandoning them?

Nightmares; flashbacks. Who has flayed her, robbed her of her skin? She is growing new skin. Scar tissue.

Sanctuary. Where is it? You create it. Living with Theo had been a sanctuary. Another person puts your ghosts, your nightmares in perspective—gives them a little less room.

*

Petra was at the prison again on the day of Hazel's release. They embraced in silence. A guard whistled. Hazel wanted to punch him. Petra noticed the hatred in her daughter's eyes. And she, too, wanted to punch the guard, punch the thick, deaf, useless walls. They got into Petra's car.

"Let me drive," Hazel said. She had not forgotten how it hurt her mother to grip the wheel. They traded places.

"Where are we going?" Petra did not want to take anything for granted.

"Home. I'm sorry. And I'm sorry for leaving you with all the animals." Hazel began to shake.

"Pull over, Schätzle." Petra had tears in her eyes as well, matches coming close to a parched wilderness. Hazel had not heard the endearment since she was very small. Though she knew her mother was able to read German, she never spoke it and perhaps no longer could.

Hazel pulled into the first gas station she saw and parked to the side of the mini mart. She let her head collapse on the steering wheel, which made her wince in pain. Her eye was still bruised. Hazel had never felt rage before, but she felt it now coming up through her like an explosion of smoke through a chimney.

Petra thought, they have broken her. If they have broken my daughter I will kill them. I will kill everything. She touched Hazel's back, gingerly at first, then began rubbing it in small circles. Hazel was bent forward, quiet and stiff under her mother's crippled hand. At the moment, Petra felt only the pain of knowing that no matter how much love managed to pass from her fingers, she could not protect her daughter's soul.

Hazel lay on the bed stroking Nolan, who had reclaimed his old spot. Theo and Claire were back in the guest room, and this time Job had followed. Hazel was talking with Sam. They would meet in Maine. Have some time together in the cabin, at the beach.

Theo sat on the edge of the bed holding Claire, waiting for Hazel to get off the phone. They had not had much time to talk. Hazel had gotten back just the day before and had wanted to be alone. She'd spent most of the day soaking in the bathtub.

Hazel put down the phone and looked at Theo. Her face had changed—and not just because of the swollen eye. It was the short hair, oddly, that made Theo feel as though she'd lost the Hazel she knew.

"You don't have to talk about it."

"It was only a week of my life. It's over," Hazel said bravely.

"Come on, Hazel, give us a break."

"That's what I'm trying to do."

"OK. Do you want to go for a walk?"

"Sure."

They walked through the field Theo had trudged through in the snow when she was pregnant. Now Claire was strapped to her front. It was a warm, you could say perfect, summer morning. They stopped at the barn. Hazel acknowledged each animal; Arches and most of the chickens were there, even Sun was still hopping around, but the old goat had died recently, while Theo and Hazel were gone. They stopped at Simon's grave. Theo picked a handful of wildflowers and put them beside the stone. She led the way into the woods. She'd had to sign the death certificate not long after she'd held her son. She held him until his flesh, still warm from being inside her, began to cool. She signed without looking.

They'd needed permission to bury Simon at the edge of the woods. Some grief is beyond words. Whatever sentimentality Theo had left in her made quick exit. She will always thank Simon for that—for the veil he lifted. He will always be her prince. Perhaps you think that is senti-mental. No. It is a fact. There are great loves you know only an instant or, in this case, nine months. Cut the umbilical cord. End of story.

"What are you going to do now?" Theo asked, moving the branches of a very young maple aside so they could pass.

"I'm not sure. I think I'll spend some time with Sam. Go back to school. Help my mother out. Keep working for the organization. Diane said she was willing to take me back. In other words, basically what I was doing before—but better. And you?" Hazel picked a purple clover and handed it to Claire.

"Diane *willing* to take you back? Give me a break. The prima donna. What did she risk in this whole enterprise? She's taking advantage of you, Hazel, can't you see that?"

"Don't worry. Don't think I haven't learned anything."

"Good."

"And you, what are you going to do?"

"Finish my degree, get work, be a mother."

"You could do those things here."

"I could."

They said nothing for a while and walked past a stand of birch trees.

"Your mother told me about a small place for rent just a few miles from here. I went to look at it. A really cozy little farmhouse."

They stood in a clearing, the grating of a chainsaw just starting in the distance.

Hazel offered her open hand to Claire, who immediately chose a finger and held on tight.

Epilogue

Hazel called her first film *Slaughterhouse Fugue* and dedicated it to the memory of her grandparents, Liam and Nora. She worried that some of the text would be too long and people wouldn't take the time to read it. Commercial size bits, Diane had advised, but this was not what Hazel wanted to do. In this film some frames are held a long time, and there is no music.

The broad back of a man is moving up and down and from side to side, rhythmically. The camera slips to his high boots, a concrete floor. Another, smaller pair of boots and up again, the camera briefly out of control, moving too fast to retain an image.

It finds a bug-infested heap in the corner. Who or what is it? A moment of not knowing and then, clearly, it is a downed cow, very like the one Hazel and Theo saw in the video they watched together at the farm. But this one is another.

The downer is too heavy to get up. She cries as a chain is attached to her leg and a winch drags her along the ground to a truck. I can see her skin rubbing off, and her bones grinding into the pavement. I can see the white of exposed bone and blood. She can't lift her head up, so her head, ear and eye start to tear on the stone. I watch the man operating the winch, and he looks impatient. I start to think of school songs, so my eyes still see but my brain is occupied. At school, we sang those grinding religious ditties: "there is a green hill far way."

As I reach the truck, the cow rolls over, exposing her udders, which are full of milk. This is the total degradation of a life.

Sue Coe, *Dead Meat*, 1995

An image of a slunk calf, and another. All on a pile. The film is black and white, but you know where the blood is. Body after body. Each unique. Alive then dead. They are right-side up, walking, then pushed, prodded, and then they are hanging like laundry, upside down. There are rows of eyes looking, then gone.

All of these were sinister incidents; but they were trifles compared to what Jurgis saw with his own eyes before long. One curious thing he had noticed, the very first day, in his profession of shoveler of guts; which was the sharp trick of the floor-bosses whenever there chanced to come a "slunk" calf. Any man who knows anything about butchering knows that the flesh of a cow that is about to calve, or has just calved, is not fit for food. A good many of these came every day to the packing-houses—and, of course, if they had chosen, it would have been an easy matter for the packers to keep them until they were fit for food. But for the saving of time and fodder, it was the law that cows of that sort came along with the others, and whoever noticed it would tell the boss, and the boss would start up a conversation with the government inspector, and the two would stroll away. So in a trice the carcass of the cow would be cleaned out, and the entrails would have vanished; it was Jurgis's task to slide them into the trap, calves and all, and on the floor below they took out these "slunk" calves and butchered them for meat, and used even the skins of them.

Upton Sinclair, *The Jungle*, 1906

A shot of the floor again, her splattered boots. Her feet move closer to the camera lens, perhaps because she is keeling over. The cries of the animals and of the machinery are muffled somewhat by the inside of her jacket.

Next, there is Wall Street at rush hour, messy lines of people moving down and up the narrow streets, disappearing into buildings.

Wall Street was originally an abattoir. Blood drained from the street into the East River. The stockyard became the stock market.

Sue Coe, Dead Meat, 1995

Now the screen is split in half. On the left a child petting a calf. On the right images we've seen repeat themselves—of slunk calves, downed cows, animals hanging in rows getting their throats slit.

The animals cry out, like babies. A sound between a human baby crying and a seagull. The animals struggle upside down, and blood splays out. Five animals are bleeding and crying at once, then they are moved down the line to have their faces skinned off. Only a few feet away, a few moments away, are the alive ones—each one perfect and unique. A different face, different eyes, different in every way, each from each. And then down a bit, a dismembered bloody rag of fur eyes popping out of a splotched skull. All the same—dead parts.

Sue Coe, Dead Meat, 1995

On the left a close-up of the child's face. On the right a close-up of the calf's face. A thin black line between the two images. The din of the slaughterhouse continues until the last thirty seconds of the film, when the brown eyes of the calf and the brown eyes of the child are accompanied only by silence and whatever sounds we happen to be making.

About the Author

Caroline Sulzer grew up in New York and in Germany. Her poetry has appeared or is forthcoming in *Calyx, Delaware Poets Anthology, Puckerbrush Review, Wolfmoon Journal* and other publications. *In the Disappearing Water* is her first novel. She currently lives in Maine with her husband, David, her two children, Jasper and Iris, and four four-legged companions.